Highland
Obligation

Highland Pride, Book 5

Highland
Obligation

Highland Pride,
Book 5

Lori Ann Bailey

Entangled Publishing, LLC
2614 South Timberline Road
Suite 105, PMB 159
Fort Collins, CO 80525
rights@entangledpublishing.com

Amara is an imprint of Entangled Publishing, LLC.

Edited by Robin Haseltine
Cover design by EDH Graphics
Cover photography by KillionGroup, 123rf, and Deposit Photos

Manufactured in the United States of America

First Edition September 2019

For Preston, I cherish the years of joy your amazing smile and quick wit have brought to our family. You have become a man of loyalty, compassion, and grace and we know the world is a better place because you are in it. Enjoy your senior year. Your dad and I love you, always, Mom.

Chapter One

CAIRNTAY CASTLE
ISLE OF SKYE, SCOTLAND
JULY, 1643

"Nae, I willnae marry." Isobel MacLean reached into her skirts for the dagger she kept hidden there. Upon finding nothing, she remembered her family had divested her of all her weapons before they'd reached the Isle of Skye's rocky shores. They had claimed this was a peaceful negotiation, and she would dishonor their clan by taking her knife into the MacDonald keep.

Her father, mother, and three brothers stood between her and the only exit from the tower room where she currently found herself sequestered. She hadn't felt this helpless since the day she and her maid had been attacked. Her heart beat so fast that it thudded in her ears.

"Aye, ye will." Her father and laird of the MacLean clan, Duncan MacLean, stared at her with a determination she had not seen since he'd ordered her brothers to discover who was behind the raids on their lands last year. Knowing her pleas to him would go unheard, she let her gaze travel to her mother, who had given up on turning her into a lady years earlier.

Amused dark brown eyes, matching her own, stared back at her. "Dinnae look at me like that. 'Tis time ye are wed." Her mother's smile indicated she was pleased with Isobel's current predicament.

Och, there would be no help from her, either.

"'Tis for the best, Isobel. He can keep ye safe." Ross, the youngest of her older brothers, implored. He must have guessed she would have turned her pleading to him next and he was correct. He usually gave in to her wishes. Because, of all people, he knew best why she couldn't leave her safety in the hands of someone else.

"I dinnae need anyone to protect me." She stood taller.

Her oldest brother, Marcus, rolled his eyes and stepped sideways to block her hasty dash toward the door.

"Ye have gotten yerself in trouble, and with the MacDonald clan is the best place ye could be." Her father's words were a slap to her already bruised pride, but she faced him and held her chin high.

The MacLean laird fisted his hands on his hips and glared at her with the accusation he'd somehow managed to keep hidden on the journey here. She had expected to hear what plans might be in place to block the Scottish Parliament from forming an alliance with the English Parliament, which was starting a civil war with King Charles. The information would be useful to the rebel group she fought alongside. If she'd had an inkling of what they'd intended for her, she never would have accompanied them to the MacDonald stronghold on the Isle of Skye.

"And ye think to leave me here without my weapons?" Her chest ached as if the air had been stripped from her lungs.

"No one would dare attack the MacDonalds."

Hah. Her father was mistaken. She would, if it guaranteed her freedom.

"So 'tis one of them ye expect me to honor?"

"Aye," her father returned.

"We dinnae even ken if The MacDonald is a true Royalist."

"Where did ye hear such nonsense? Ye ken he is."

"Their laird kept ye captive in their dungeons only a couple of moons ago. Have ye forgotten?"

How could her father do such a thing after what the MacDonalds had put them through? Ross had nearly lost his life trying to save him.

"Nae, I ken very well what kind of man Alastair MacDonald is. And I ken he and his clan will do whatever it takes to keep one of their own safe. 'Tis why ye will become one of them." Her father folded his arms and looked down on her with darkened eyes that said he was done with the conversation.

Balling her fists, she pinned her father with all the courage she had in her. "I willnae do it."

"Ye will or ye will bring dishonor to our clan."

Guilt stabbed her. Since her father had already made the arrangements, it would be true.

"I should have been consulted."

"Ye never would have agreed."

Precisely her point. She inhaled sharply and glared at her father with the most defiance she could muster. She felt like a cat surrounded by rabid dogs bent on her destruction, never mind that they were her family and thought they were helping her. In actuality, they were taking everything from her by forcing her into marriage, especially one that would keep her secreted away on an island, separated from the very land and people she'd been fighting to protect.

"Then why do ye expect me to do so now?"

It was Ross who stepped forward. "Because Grant MacDonald is a good man, and he will be kind to ye."

"Grant MacDonald. Is he no' the man who thinks there can be peace between the Royalists and Covenanters? Ye would wed me to someone who doesnae even fight for the cause?" She was so mad she could spit. She had nothing in common with a man who would seek a truce between the men who were suppressing her people.

"'Tis the best option, since it is rumored that Argyll kens who ye are. If the Covenanter leader finds ye, he will keep ye alive only to torture ye until ye can no longer take it," Ross pleaded.

So, Ross had had a hand in this deal. He'd always felt guilty about letting her and her maid down that day. The afternoon she'd discovered the only person she could rely on was herself. The day she had changed.

True, she should have done a better job hiding her identity and her activities as second-in-command of the Royalist Resistance. The band was the only group of rebels brave enough to stand up for those repressed by the Covenanters, who supported the agreement with the English Parliament and the Puritan Roundheads. If those people got their way, Royalists like her clan, who were Catholic and supported King Charles, would be forced to convert. She'd joined their ranks to save her family from such tyranny. Now, the way of life she'd come to know was in jeopardy.

If she left now, she might be able to track down the man who had recognized her during the most recent skirmish, dispatching swift justice on him and ensuring her well-being. But before she'd been able to strike down Torsten Campbell, a massive brute of a man in the Royalist party she'd been helping protect had turned his rage on her, yelling something about her interference. Men never thought a woman could wield anything heavier than a knitting needle. She had ignored him then skirted around only to discover Torsten had escaped.

Most likely the foolish man was hunting for her instead of blabbering. He likely wouldn't risk exposing her secret—the bounty for her capture was hefty and if someone else brought her in, he would lose the reward.

"And even if I marry the man, what is to keep me here?" she asked.

"Ye will stay with yer husband." Her father's words intruded.

Maybe if she pretended to be a meek, obedient wife she could sneak off and take care of the threat. There was no way out of the arrangement at this point. For now, she could go along with it until her family was gone.

A light rapping reached her ears. Ross turned and peeked through the door. Apparently satisfied with what he saw, he pulled it in to admit a bevy of maids with silks and grooming instruments.

"Och, ye cannae be serious?" Her throat tightened at the prospect of what they were about to do.

"Aye. Ye will go into this marriage looking like a proper woman."

But she knew what her father was really saying: *Yer days with the Resistance are done.* But for her, it wasn't that simple.

Meek wife, bide yer time, family will leave, she repeated to herself

"Well," she said as her brothers and father stood waiting for her objections. "I cannae prepare if ye are in here. Please leave."

Before doing so, Ross circled the room; she assumed to check for any weapons or means of escape, but she'd already looked everywhere. The only way in and out was the well-guarded door. They had not even brought her trunks into the room. If they had, she'd have been able to take the dagger hidden inside and cut enough fabric to scale down the tower wall.

They'd even lied to get her to this island to begin with, telling her they were going to discuss strategies for eliminating the Covenanter threats in the Highlands. It was a prospect they knew she couldn't pass up. She should have known her family wouldn't have included her or brought her lady mother along.

They were all opposed to her position with the Royalist Resistance. And this had been their plan to remove her from that life.

Seeming satisfied she had no means of escape, Ross nodded at the rest of her family, and they filed out of the room.

Hours later, after being fed, bathed, and forced into a dress so soft and silky it slid over her skin, tickling and leaving her feeling vulnerable, she found herself being escorted down the halls of a cold stone castle that would soon become her home. Her heart hammered. Ross threaded his arm through hers and drew her down the corridors until they stood in front of two large, ornately carved, wooden doors. They alluded to the strength and prominence of the MacDonald clan and made her want to turn and run, seek shelter where no one could find her.

The portals swung in to reveal a packed chapel. As all heads turned to face her, Ross guided her to the altar. She didn't recognize anyone.

Anonymity. Relief washed over her until her eyes rested on the man at the front of the room, Grant MacDonald, her betrothed. Her steps faltered. Her soon-to-be husband was the man from the battle who had let Torsten Campbell get away.

• • •

Nae.

Grant's hands fisted as he caught a glimpse of his new bride. His eyes must be playing tricks on him. He was supposed to be wedding the MacLean laird's daughter, Isobel. This was the wench from the Royalist Resistance. As she moved closer, he was certain it was the woman he'd seen wielding a sword in battle, but the laird's heir escorted her down as if she were a lady of worth. He swallowed.

The famed fighter had kept her identity hidden for years, and now he saw how. No one would suspect a cultured, refined woman to be donning men's clothes and sneaking off with wanted criminals.

He'd already lost one wife, what would it say about him if he killed his second on their wedding night?

The lass's gaze skidded across the crowd to land on his and shock registered in her stare just as her feet stalled and her brother tugged her along. Aye, she recognized him as well. Good, because she had a lot to answer for.

Why had he not insisted on meeting his betrothed before the ceremony? If he'd known whom he was about to marry, he'd have found a way out of it.

But the MacLeans had been delayed in getting to his home on the Isle of Skye and had insisted the wedding plans go ahead as they were. Had it been The MacLean's strategy all along to dump his lioness of a daughter onto a man who might be able to control her? Did the man even know the extent of his daughter's activities?

Isobel MacLean was bonny in the candlelight, dressed in white, hair pinned in place, a deceptively sedate smile plastered on her face. But even if she cleaned up nicely, he would never forget the lass he blamed for the death of his friend.

The closer she got, the surer he became that she was the only female member of the Royalist Resistance, the group who had taken it upon themselves to seek retribution against the Covenanters who spread their own vicious brand of hatred around the Highlands. Neither group was better than the other.

His stomach churned and he looked to his father, thinking one more time to beg his way out of this marriage, but the pleading he'd already done had fallen on deaf ears. His father had falsely imprisoned The MacLean, and this was their clan's demand for reparation. Denying his bride at this point would start a war. Wedding the MacLean lass was his duty, whether she fit the mold of what he wanted or not.

He'd heard rumors about The MacLean's only daughter, how she acted more like a man than a woman, how she never dressed for social occasions and how she shunned the traditional female role. He'd passed the tales off as gossip or jealousy because it was also said that despite her habits, she was an attractive lass.

Those rumors had been true as well. She was lovely, but he'd known that the first moment he'd seen her in the middle of a skirmish between Covenanters and the Royalist Resistance. She had been confident and her face flushed a rosy pink from exertion. An overwhelming urge to protect her had overcome him. It's what had distracted him from his duty and led to his friend's death. And then she'd cursed him, not even thankful for his assistance.

It only now made sense that she would be one of the Earl of Argyll's most wanted. If the leader of the Covenanters discovered who she was, it would bring all the man's forces down onto his people. Grant clenched his hands and tried to bring his anger in check.

She'd be his responsibility now. Her days of causing conflicts in the Highlands were over, even if he had to keep her locked away in the dungeons of Cairntay.

Ross MacLean put Isobel's hands in his and nodded, backing away and leaving the two alone in the front of the room with the priest. Grant squeezed a little too hard and she glared at him then wiggled her fingers, trying to break free.

Leaning in, she whispered in his ear, "Ye are hurting me."

"Ye are lucky there is a room full of witnesses and a man of God or I would be using strong language to express my feelings about your recent activities." Still, he eased his grip.

His gaze darted to his father, who looked pleased. Maybe the man mistook their banter as acceptance of this farce of a union. He had to admit Isobel was a fine sight. But his father hadn't seen her dressed as a man wielding a sword as if she had been bred to battle.

"I dinnae want this any more than ye do," she retorted as she pushed at the stray golden-brown curl which bobbed down from the top of her temple.

"I doubt that." Rage bubbled up as he studied her eyes and remembered those of his fallen friend.

"Then release me from this match," she hissed as he caught a whiff of exotic flowers that heated his blood and stirred his loins.

"And start a war with yer clan? I think no'."

She tried to pull free, but he tightened his grip just as the priest coughed to get their attention.

What felt like hours later, the priest instructed him to kiss his bride as cheers erupted from the room. His body heated as he glanced down into her brown eyes, ones that were now focused intently on him as her lips parted in surrender or shock. He guessed neither of them had remembered this part was coming. He felt drawn in like a ship caught in a strong current.

He dipped his head to do what was required of him, but

when their lips touched, he found hers soft and pliant. Isobel inhaled as if she'd been without air for weeks. Her hand grasped onto his arm and her sweet, exotic scent flooded his nostrils. For a brief moment, he wanted to deepen the embrace but a jeer from nearby brought him back. He pulled away.

Then, he was gripping his bride's long slender fingers as he hauled her down the middle of the chapel, out the door, and to the nearest empty room. As he pushed open the library doors, he was greeted with the familiar scents of stale papers, smoke, and strong spirits, but they did nothing to tamp down the rage that had surfaced at seeing Isobel MacLean's—no, Isobel MacDonald's—face. Swinging her around to let go of the viper, he turned and bolted the door.

"Ye will cease yer activities with that group right away."

"And ye think just because I am forced to wed ye I will do what ye ask." She was a good four or five inches shorter than him, but she straightened her shoulders, tilted her chin up, and met his stare with no fear.

"Aye. I am yer husband and ye will obey me."

"I obey no one," came her curt reply. She stood, hands on hips, feet spread shoulder-width apart, not in the least intimidated by his rage. She should be, because it frightened him that he could be so angry with anyone.

"Ye are now my obligation, and ye will follow my orders."

She crossed the small space between them to stand right in front of him. The top of her head came up to his nose, but her stare made it appear as if she were looking down at him. The lass didn't even blink. And while he'd never assaulted a woman, she had no way of knowing what kind of man he was. She must be daft.

"I will do as I please."

His fingers clasped the fabric on her shoulders, holding firm to make his point. "Dinnae force me to keep ye locked away." Through the thin material, he felt well-muscled arms, tense and on alert, giving away what she kept hidden. She did have some sense of preservation somewhere in that thick skull of hers. She shuddered then tilted her head higher.

But he was distracted when the pink tip of Isobel's tongue darted out to wet her lips and she swallowed. A light pounding started in his chest; it got louder, and he realized it was a rapping on the door.

His father called out, "Grant. Ye and yer bride are wanted in the great hall for a toast."

Closing his lids, he blocked her out for a moment and took a deep breath. He was the MacDonald heir and had a duty. Opening his eyes, his gaze was drawn to the slight curve of her neck. She had glanced away and was scanning the room, probably looking for some means of escape.

Letting his hands slide down her arms, he took one hand and pulled her toward the door. Suddenly he was afraid to let her out of his sight, like she would flee if he didn't keep a close enough watch on her. At the movement, her focus returned to him and her eyes dilated. He wanted to believe it was with desire, but it might actually be fear, and he wondered if the instinct to run had taken over. "Ye will stay by my side until we can finish this conversation."

Her gaze darkened as defiance returned, but she didn't protest when he opened the door and drew her out into the hall, guiding them toward the crowd waiting to see the happy couple.

Chapter Two

Isobel's new husband pulled her through the cheering crowd toward the dais at the opposite end of the great hall. The movement thankfully shook free the odd stirrings his nearness had caused. The chamber was so large, she almost felt as if she were outside at twilight as the sun dribbled in through windows stained with blues, greens, and reds. The blazing colors imbued a sense of magic to the space. She attempted to ignore the majesty of the place and concentrate on the faces. These people looked friendly enough. If only they knew how she wished to be anywhere but here, maybe then they would let her leave.

She concentrated on not tripping on the silly gown she'd been forced to wear, cursing herself for actually liking the way it slid across her skin and how the fabric glowed in the tranquil light of the room, shimmering like pearls. She pushed away the thrill that her husband might find her appealing in the garment. *Och*, it was because his eyes were a bonny shade of blue that had distracted her the first time she'd seen him. And that was the reason she was in this mess. She'd been enthralled by the brawny man who'd been looking out for her safety the day she'd been identified. If she hadn't been thwarted, Torsten never would have gotten away.

They took the steps up to a long table already filled with people. The scene reminded her that, at one time, she'd been an innocent, naive child who had wanted this—a marriage and to be nothing more than a happy bride. Buried emotions pricked at the back of her eyes. She couldn't wait to get this gown off and burn it.

Her heart stopped and her steps faltered. Would this angry beast beside her want to bed her tonight?

She claimed her seat and Grant slid in beside her, finally letting go of the confining grip on her hand. Her gaze drifted farther down the table to notice her mother's smile. Was it relief she saw there? Emilia had always wished for her to be a lady. When that dream had been taken from Isobel, she'd squashed it for her mother, too, by becoming who she was now.

Her husband's hand landed on her leg. She flinched. His grip was firm but not overbearing, a reminder she was no longer free. Her skin tingled.

Pivoting toward the man beside her, she was struck by his calm presence despite the currents she knew waged war beneath his facade. That's what had drawn her interest the last time they'd met in the thick of battle. All one had to do was glance upon his sapphire eyes to know he was born to be a leader.

Her thoughts again turned to the bedding, and heat crawled through her limbs. She wasn't small, but Grant MacDonald was a large man. She had managed to keep her maidenhood this long because Alex Gordon, the leader of the Resistance, warned his men off her and because she always kept a knife at her side. Looking down at the table, she spied one just to the side of her trencher. Although it was dull and not meant for combat, she couldn't help but smile as relief flooded her senses.

Grant's hand held her under the table as if to keep her secured to his side should she decide to flee. His grip lessened and fingers slid up her sensitive skin as she fought back the gooseflesh rising in their wake; she kept her own hands studiously clasped in her lap. Glancing over at him, she met a stern, knowing gaze. Her husband shook his head, then his hand left her arm long enough to take the dirk from in front of her. He placed it out of reach before returning the vise-like grip on her leg.

The horde of MacDonalds quieted as their laird stood and raised his cup in the air. "To new beginnings and a renewed commitment between the MacDonalds and MacLeans to protect each other and the Highlands."

Leaning in toward Grant, she gritted out behind teeth she hoped looked like a smile, "How am I to ensure the Highlands are safe if ye willnae let me leave?"

"'Tis no' yer job to cause more conflict among our people." Disapproval, perhaps even anger, darkened his gaze as it pinned her.

Is that what he thought of the Resistance?

He was wrong. "I am protecting our people."

"Ye are a fool if ye choose to believe yer mischief is helping anyone."

She sucked in, absorbing his words like a physical blow.

Her father stood up. "To a union blessed with peace and prosperity." She wanted to add "based on treachery and misery" to her father's list, but held her tongue as she raised her glass and took a long sip of the surprisingly smooth ale.

Overhearing Grant's father speak, she turned to see whom he was addressing. "Ye dinnae have to leave so soon."

"Aye. 'Tis best we were on our way at first light. The Macnabs seem to be eager to sign the Covenants, and I dinnae wish to leave our land vulnerable to traitorous neighbors." Isobel had to struggle to hear her father over the throng's noise, but she recognized the name of the clan whose loyalty was still in doubt. Thankfully, she was adept at reading lips.

"We'll also be sending a delegation to Edinburgh to make a case against the Covenant before 'tis written into law."

She couldn't see or hear The MacDonald's reply.

So, her family was deserting her at first light. If she was careful, she might be able to sneak out and stow aboard the ship that carried them to the other side of the fast-flowing waters that separated her from mainland Scotland. If she was caught, though, they would bring her straight back, and her horrid husband might make true on his promise to see her to the dungeons.

Was her freedom worth the risk? Glancing up, she caught her husband's all too knowing glare as he shook his head.

"What?" She straightened her shoulders and attempted to look demure and innocent.

"Dinnae even think of whatever ye are planning."

Argh, she wanted to kick him under the table.

The rest of the meal she ate quietly, focusing on retaining her strength and coming up with a plan. If she did run and seek shelter with other Royalists in the Highlands, would the MacDonalds hold her clan responsible? Aye, they most likely would, since she was now wed to the laird's heir. Half the Highlands would be hunting her to return her while the half that favored the Covenanters would still be after the bounty on her head.

When her husband stood and dragged her up alongside him, a thunderous roar erupted. Her ears ringing, she fisted her free hand, aware for the first time that she didn't want to be alone with Grant.

"I would like another cup of ale." She tried to sit back down, but he coiled an arm around her waist and held her tight, as if they were lovers and wanted to be together.

"I'll have one brought up for ye." He pulled her from the room as a group followed behind them chanting something about the bedding. She chose to ignore the bawdy words.

Grant led her down the hall to a flight of stone steps, and she struggled to keep from tripping on the hem of her gown as he urged her onward. It was dark, but by the light of the sconces she could make out the stairs as she trailed her free hand up the smooth rock of the unfamiliar walls. Walking toward the end of the new hall she found herself in, she noticed a second flight of stairs down the back side of the castle.

Her husband stopped at the door just before her projected means of escape. Pushing the solid wood, he let go of her hand and indicated she should enter. Stepping forward, she remembered something she'd heard years ago as a child, something she'd thought never to need. Never enter the bedchamber on your wedding night with your left foot. Too late she realized what she was doing and pivoted back around to stop her progression, bumping into her husband and earning a growl from him.

"We dinnae need more bad luck than we already have," she snapped at him.

Surprising her, his face softened. "I agree."

Arms wound around her back and thighs to pick her up and carry her over the threshold. *Och*, this was not what she'd had in mind. Still, she felt light and feminine cradled in the silk and his arms. Something in her fluttered. Argh, she was weak. She would not let marriage turn her into some simpering lass who couldn't take care of herself.

Once in the chamber, her gaze skimmed the large room to see candles had already been lit. A woman she'd seen at the ceremony and then dinner sat in a chair awaiting their arrival. The woman floated toward them, all grace and poise.

"Ye can put me down now." She hated the hitch in her breath and the throaty sound of the words.

His blue gaze dropped to hers and he held her a moment longer, his studious expression contemplating something about her that apparently vexed him. Good. She would continue to be a thistle poking at him until he realized this arrangement was not going to work.

Before she could insist that he let her go, the woman spoke, "Welcome to the family. May I call ye Isobel?"

Grant straightened and let her slide from his arms. "This is my mother, Fenella."

She wobbled when her husband released her, but it had to be because of the fancy slippers she wore. It had nothing to do with the glide down his hard-muscled thigh or the sensations that remained on her flesh where his arms had held her. Nodding, she resisted the inclination to reach out and touch his leg to make sure she was mistaken by the strength she'd imagined there.

Instead, she returned the pleasant woman's smile. "Aye, 'tis fine. Thank ye."

Looking to her son, Fenella gave a knowing grin. "I have sprinkled and blessed the bed."

"'Twas nae need for it. It didnae work last time."

Last time? Heat stole onto her cheeks as gooseflesh rose on her arms.

Grant's mother waved away his remark then started speaking before Isobel could voice any concerns. "We had yer things brought up earlier. Yer gowns have been hung." Fenella nodded to the corner of the room, and Isobel followed the woman's movements.

"Thank ye." Gowns. What gowns?

"I'll leave ye two alone now." Fenella grinned at her son with a proud gaze and, for a moment, Isobel was jealous. She couldn't remember the last time her own mother had given her such a look. Then Fenella looked upon her with a warm and genuine expression. "We are truly happy to have ye here."

Isobel's head bobbed in acknowledgment but no words came out. Her mother-in-law walked to the door.

Wait, she wanted to scream out.

She didn't want to be alone with her husband. She didn't have a weapon other than her hands, but they would be no match against this mountain of a man, should she wish to use them. Shifting, she started toward her trunks to make sure her knives were still hidden inside, but she stopped once she got closer. These weren't her chests.

Her head started to hum as a request behind her registered. "Will ye have someone bring up another cup of ale, please."

Well, he was nice to his mother, at least. What did he have against her?

Lifting up the first lid, she nearly choked on the bile that rose from somewhere deep inside. Slippers and stockings. She opened the second, which was filled with linen shifts. A piece of paper lay on top. Her fingers shook as she lifted it and read the words in her mother's handwriting.

Dearest Isobel,

It is time for ye to become the woman ye are supposed to be. The MacDonalds are honorable, hard-working people and they will take good care of you. Please ken that we love ye.

Ye are always in our hearts,
Father & Mother

After balling up the letter, she tossed it back in the trunk and slammed the lid. How long had they planned to abandon her here?

Once she stood and turned around, she found her husband staring at her. "Did they take all yer weapons?"

Anger sparked. How had he guessed?

She should lie to him. Tell him he'd never find where she had them hidden, but he was just the type of man who would rip everything apart until he found them. He might not believe her and do it anyway. *Hell*, did she even care if he tore it all up? She just might do it herself.

"They took it all."

Her shoulders drooped as all her hopes fled. Who would she be now? And who was this man she was married to?

"Ye ken who I am. Tell me something about ye." She made an attempt to start a conversation, although even she could hear that her tone came across as one of an angry child instead of a lady trying to woo her husband.

"I am the man who is now forced to save ye from yerself."

If she'd had her dirk, she would have flung it at him.

Instead, ignoring the barb, she walked to the window. This room was overlooking the cliff. There was just enough land at the bottom that she might be able to climb down, but it was a long way and she might break her neck trying. But, even if she did escape at this point, where would she go? She was on a bloody island.

Grant came to stand behind her. She hadn't heard or seen him, but she could sense his presence. It was as if the air obeyed when he moved. He might be used to people doing his bidding, but he would learn quickly she didn't bow to intimidation.

Turning, she glowered at him. "I dinnae wish to give my body to ye." He needed to know she would put up a fight.

His lip quirked. "There is nothing about ye that makes me want to take ye to my bed."

Her heart lurched and stuttered. Why did his comment sting? "Then ye shall give me a separate room."

Hope blossomed.

"Nae."

Hope faded.

Skirting around him, she moved to the chair, eased down and removed her slippers, confident she was safe, at least for the evening. She didn't know much about her new husband, but he did seem to be a man of his word and didn't appear to be interested in what little she possessed in the way of womanly charm. A bit of her couldn't help but cry out on the inside, though. Despite his disdain for her, she'd liked the way his hand felt in hers as he'd drawn her to this room. A man had never before held her so gently.

Standing, she took a deep breath and cursed the gown her family had forced her to don. The awful thing was already turning her back into the naive girl she was before. Making matters worse, the ties were in the back. She could just sleep in it, but would toss and turn so much she would find herself tangled in it all night.

"Will ye please help me with the ribbons?"

He visibly stiffened and swallowed. The arse. He was more interested in her than he let on. Or, he truly was repulsed by her.

She might have blushed, but she turned so he could not see. Then there was that presence again, right behind her, not moving, but demanding the attention of everything around him. She waited, and his fingers were pulling and loosening the bindings on her gown. Her skin tingled at the attentions.

"Did ye bring a maid to help ye with such tasks?" His angry tone from before had smoothed to one she couldn't quite name. The tenor was husky and strained.

"Nae, my family didnae even tell me I was coming to be sold." Maybe she should try to dull her tongue as well. Grant hadn't seemed to have much of an option in the arrangement, either.

"I will find ye one then."

"Nae." She spun abruptly, her breath coming faster as her previous maid's accusations beat in her head. She could not be responsible for another one. "I didnae have a maid at home. I dinnae want one."

"Even if it means relying on yer husband to dress and undress ye every day?" His lip twitched as if he was either disgusted with the idea of helping her or intrigued by his suggestion. She chose not to entertain either idea.

"I will find clothes that dinnae require it." She folded her arms over her chest.

Grant backed and she waited for him to turn before she pulled the soft fabric over her head and placed it on the nearest chair. Dressed only in her shift, she bolted toward her new bed and slid in before her husband had the chance to turn back around, drawing the covers up to her chin. The scent of cedar after a fresh rain filled her nostrils. Grant's smell. She wanted to inhale deeper and learn it, but instead she jerked the blankets back down to her chest.

She needed rest if she was to attempt to escape tomorrow.

• • •

Not yet ready to crawl into bed with the viper, Grant kicked off his boots. He pulled up a chair and studied his new wife as she tossed and turned, her brown hair still pulled up in pins. She was nothing like Lyall. His first wife had been perfect, a petite blonde. She had been quiet and obedient, always looking for a way to please and keep peace in their marriage bed.

This wife was the complete opposite and not at all what he wanted.

His thoughts turned to what he should be doing on his wedding night. *Hell*, he wasn't opposed to sleeping with the lass who now occupied his space; she was well built, sleek, and muscled. Aye, he'd peeked when she removed her gown. How could he not?

It was like during the skirmish when he'd spied her large brown eyes. There was a fire in the depths of them, a spark that had called to him and had him enthralled. Although she'd worn men's clothing, there had been no mistaking her curves or the gentle lift in her chin. He'd had the sudden urge to cart her away, protect her from the sights and sounds of the carnage that surrounded them.

And for a brief moment as her eyes had locked with his, they'd both been mesmerized. The noise around them had disappeared and all he saw was her. He had let down his guard completely because of his attraction to her, and that was something a leader could never do.

And then he noticed the lass wielded a sword some men would have trouble lifting. His quick appraisal had warned him she was dangerous, but something had made him want to get to know her better, shield her from the devastation that was raining down on them. Now, while watching her sleep, he was reminded that his lack of judgment in that moment was what had gotten his friend killed.

After he'd helped to bury Tomas, he'd searched for any information he could find on the famed lass who fought with the Royalist Resistance. He'd not been able to discover much because her identity was a closely guarded secret. But tales of her prowess with a weapon were legend, and Argyll had offered an award for anyone who could bring her in, dead or alive.

Isobel was a danger to him, his clan, and herself.

She'd settled and his neck was starting to ache. Rising, he undressed and strolled to the bed before he remembered the way Isobel had eyed the dirk on the table at dinner. It was probably prudent to make sure she didn't have access to the kitchens until he was certain the wench wouldn't kill him.

After moving back to the heavy wooden chair he'd just left, he picked it up and placed it by the door, just under the latch. She would have to slide it across the floor if she intended to leave, and he was a light sleeper. Just in case, he retrieved the table and put it there as well. Satisfied she wouldn't be able to sneak out during the evening, he made his way back to the bed, slid under the covers, and shut his eyes.

Damn. He could smell her again and she'd fallen straight into slumber as if she had already come to trust him. Fighting the urge to reach over and caress her skin, just to see if it was as soft as it looked, he crossed his arms over his chest.

Waking in the early morning hours, Grant found his wife had turned and faced him. He studied her placid features, rounded cheeks, and long lashes. Despite the rumors of her being more man than woman, she was quite attractive with full wine-kissed lips and thick hair which had loosened from the pins and given her the disheveled look of a woman who had been thoroughly ravished. Of course it could be because she wasn't covered in mud and blood, which was how tales of her had spread through the Highlands.

What had turned such a lovely creature into the animal she appeared to be?

His groin was starting to ache, but the last thing he wanted was to wake the viper's tongue. He enjoyed her more this way. Sliding from the bed, he dressed, removed his barriers, and headed for the kitchens, stopping along the way to leave instructions for a man, no he made it two, to stand outside their room until he could return.

As he reached the bottom of the stairs, he heard voices coming from his father's study, so he rapped on the door and entered after his father called out.

He discovered his wife's parents, Duncan and Emilia MacLean, and her brothers gathered in the room. His father smiled when he entered. "Shut the door behind ye. The MacLean was just telling me that more clans are planning to sign the Covenants. It appears even the Macnabs will be sending men to England to fight against the king."

"'Tis one of the reasons we must leave straight away. We cannae leave our lands unprotected with Argyll and his men so close."

"When does Parliament vote on it?" Grant moved closer, knowing he had to do something. Too many clans were signing on to this agreement with the English Parliament.

"Mid-August." Duncan MacLean shook his head. "Montrose is planning to have a group of men stand before our Parliament to speak against the agreement with the English Parliament and their Puritans."

Grant had met James Graham, the 1st Marquess of Montrose. At one time, the man had sided with the Covenanters, but was now one of King Charles's greatest supporters and a strong leader. If there was hope for a peaceable outcome, it would be with Montrose at the helm.

"There is still a chance they may see reason, then." Grant rubbed his chin.

"Nae likely, but as long as there is a chance we'll be there to help. I'll be sending my sons to represent our clan." The MacLean shook his head.

"We must try," his father agreed. The words were met with silence, as they all most likely debated what would happen to the Royalist clans in the Highlands if they didn't find common ground with the religious zealots who had control of Parliament.

After a moment, Grant spoke up. "Do ye ken who yer daughter is?"

The MacLean's lips pursed and he gave a quick nod. The brothers looked equally ashamed. "We just discovered," the oldest one, Marcus, said.

"Who is she?" His father stared at him.

"She is the woman who fights for the Royalist Resistance." After answering his father, he turned to the MacLean. "Why did ye no' share that information?"

The youngest of the brothers, Ross, chimed in. "We thought to guard her." Shoulders straight, the man looked him dead in the eyes.

"Ye would bring war to our shores." His father stood and stared down at the men.

"Nae, we wish to bring peace to all. We believe ye are the only ones to keep her safe. If her identity is discovered, the Campbells will attack and destroy our clan. They willnae dare attack on yer shores with us to their backs. We are trusting ye with someone very dear to us. And if ye can give her a home where she feels safe, she might stop fighting."

If he could be certain she wouldn't try to return to the rebels, it would go a long way toward easing his concerns. But she had a long road to make amends for her past, and so far her actions didn't appear to be those of a woman who wished to change.

Ross continued, "The Campbells are the only Covenanters to be concerned with and if they see her as a diligent wife, no one will ever ken her past. Ye will also have strong Royalist clans surrounding yer lands. The MacLeans and Camerons to the south. And the Macnabs will surely fall on the side of the Royalists, now that their laird's health is failing and the heir will soon be chief. He just wed his sister into the Cameron clan and formed an alliance. Ye also have the MacLeods to yer north and they are staunch supporters of the king."

"Why does she do it?" Grant asked the question that had been plaguing him since the day he'd seen her wielding her sword in battle against the Covenanters.

"She feels as if she is protecting people, but in the process, she shuts out everyone who loves her." Ross gave him a tight smile. Grant had the impression guilt lay somewhere beneath his pleading gaze. Ross moved in closer so that only Grant could hear. "She has a good heart. Dinnae let her fool ye."

Shouting erupted in the hall, and Ross's shoulders drooped.

Straightening, Grant walked to the door and pulled it open to admit his new bride, who was followed closely by the guards he'd set at their door. "'Tis all right. I'll take her from here."

"Am I a prisoner?" Isobel rushed up to him, cheeks flushed, hair pulled from the pins and left free to dangle to her waist in heaps of bouncing brown curls. She looked as if he'd done those things to her that he'd fantasized about during the night, just as he'd cursed himself for thinking them.

"Nae."

She glared, brown eyes piercing him, and although he was exasperated with her already, he had the strangest desire to smile. He tamped it down as he studied her attire, a haphazardly donned deep blue gown that bunched around the bodice because the ties had not been properly secured. He had the urge to pull her in the corner and fix it or take her back up to their room and do what he should have done last night.

"Then why would they no' let me leave the room?"

He wasn't going to tell her he didn't trust her. That didn't seem the proper way to start a marriage, but surely she already knew. "I didnae want ye to get lost on yer first day here. 'Tis my intention to show ye around today." He didn't even know the thought was true until he spoke it. Although they would never have the relationship he and his previous wife had shared, she deserved to know about where she was to live.

"We will be leaving shortly," Isobel's father chimed in.

As her gaze drifted to the MacLean lairds, her hands fisted at her sides, confirming his instincts had been correct—she had planned to be on that boat with them when they left.

"Why so soon?" Her words were quiet now. Her gaze darted around the room as if in search of a new plan, a new way out.

"'Tis time we let ye ken yer new family, and we have business to take care of."

Her gaze drifted back to Grant's and she looked like a lost puppy with those big soulful eyes, but she tamped down whatever she was feeling, sticking her nose up in the air.

"We must break our fast first," his father said and gestured to the door.

"Aye." He threaded his arm through Isobel's and she flinched. She took a deep breath and nodded at him, trying to look like an obedient wife, but he saw behind those eyes. She was like a caged bird whose wings had not yet been clipped, still looking for an opportunity to fly.

Chapter Three

Isobel groaned as her only means of escape sailed toward her old home, leaving her in a place she knew nothing about. Really, though, if she'd managed to go, what would she have done? Lived on the run, underground with members of the Resistance? They weren't loyal to her, and what would they expect from a woman for a warm bed and food? She bet it would be a price she wasn't willing to pay.

When she'd first joined the group, she'd told herself it was to keep her clan safe. That was no longer her main reason for staying. With her gone, who would look after Stew? He had joined their group in the last year and was too young to be on his own. None of the men would look after him the way she had. Stew needed her.

Everything hinged on finding Torsten Campbell and ensuring he didn't give her away to Argyll. If he had already exposed her, she'd be in custody. With the price on her head so high, it would only be a matter of time before he came for her, but if he did, how could she protect herself or these people without a weapon?

"Come," Grant ordered as he eyed her with what appeared to be a mixture of resentment and curiosity.

"Where are we going?"

"Since we are stuck together, 'tis nae better time to learn about yer new home."

Nodding, she glanced to the choppy waters once more. There was something soothing about them, even though they kept her from searching out the man who might hand her over to Argyll. She didn't know the first thing about how to sail a boat. If she wanted to get back to the mainland, she'd have to somehow convince her husband to get her there.

She turned back to Grant. Studying all of him for the first time, she found him an attractive man, well-muscled and lean. Although he'd stopped her from destroying her foe on that fateful day near Edinburgh, he appeared to be competent and would one day be a good leader. "What shall we see first?"

"I think the village, then Cairntay."

She took one last look across the water, then let her gaze roam the shoreline of her new home. They were perched high on a stony cliff. Trees and full blooming bushes dotted the steep incline. She admired how the island's natural landscape lent itself to the protection of those who called it home.

Stone steps led to a small beach where boats were moored to the coast. The bobbing vessels and the residents of Skye were protected by the chopping waters that prevented enemies from the mainland making the journey without notice. At the edge of the sand, trees littered the landscape in pleasing shades of green, making her think of apples, lush grassy fields, and emeralds.

Perhaps this place did have its merits. But what threats could come from farther inland? Surveying the village sounded like a good idea, so she followed her husband.

She strolled beside him, but they kept a respectable

distance between them as they ambled away from the cliff that overlooked the water separating her from the world she knew. Anyone watching would never guess they were husband and wife. And that they had shared a bed last night.

At one point during the night, he'd rolled into her side and murmured, "I'll do it for the clan." He continued to talk, but she could only make out snatches as he'd become more restless.

She'd placed her hand on his chest, hoping to ease his troubled sleep so she could doze again. His heart raced, but his fingers came up to close around hers and he settled. The tempo within her chest had increased, because his touch was gentle yet protective, as if he counted her as part of the clan he was to lead and care for. Silly, but in that moment, she'd felt safe and was able to slide back into slumber with an ease that usually evaded her.

A flush of warmth stole up her neck, but the heat didn't make it to her cheeks. Why had he not claimed his husbandly rights last night? Did he despise her that much, or had it to do with what his mother said?

"Have ye been married before?" She shuddered. Once the words left her lips, she wanted to take them back, thinking they sounded too intimate, personal. She didn't want to get to know her husband.

"Aye." He said nothing else as a cool wind blew in from the waters at their backs, her hair whipping into her face. He seemed reluctant to share his past with her, a past with a woman he may have cared for. It was probably for the best.

Pulling her wayward tresses back, she felt her gown bunch and gap in the front, giving a nice view of the clean new shift beneath. Darn her family for taking her things and leaving her with trunks of useless dresses and frivolities she wanted no part of.

She was startled when Grant grabbed her by the shoulder

and pulled her over to the side of the path, letting others pass as she stared up into a gaze that had no right to be as bonny as the bluest of skies. Suddenly she felt…inadequate…the words from long ago coming back to haunt her. *Och, too scraggly. It looks more like a boy to me.*

It was no surprise her husband didn't want her.

But still, as his hand slid to the front of her gown and pulled at the laces she'd never bothered to learn how to tie, an odd tingle spread through her limbs and for once she wanted to be fair of face and know what it was like for a man to desire her. And she wanted to feel his lips on hers again, not be interrupted by the roar of his clan celebrating. His mouth had been soft and tender. Despite his anger at her, during that short embrace she'd felt treasured, even desired.

Hell. The salty air on this island was doing something odd to her.

"Was she bonny?" Foolish, so foolish and lack-witted. How could she ask a question like that, and why did she care?

"Who?"

"Yer first wife."

"Aye," he said, his face darkening as if she'd insulted him.

Of course she was, she thought, a knife stabbing into her chest. She'd never wanted to marry, but if she had, she would have wanted to be the one who made her partner's world complete. Another woman had beaten her to the heart of her husband, even if she'd stood a chance.

"What happened to her?" A lump caught in her throat as he finished tying off the knot and turned away.

"An illness took her."

"I'm sorry." And she truly meant it, because it was obviously painful for him. Despite their predicament, she suspected him to be a good man.

"'Twas a long time ago." He married young then. *Och*, but he'd be expected to produce heirs. A chill from a new burst of wind made her shudder.

"Do ye have any bairn?" She couldn't stop the questions leaping from her mouth.

"Nae."

Trees near the edge of the clearing swayed and their leaves rustled in the breeze that gentled as their distance from the shore increased. Their appendages danced and swished in a soothing pattern, reminding her of evenings spent falling asleep, camped near deep brown trunks of strong timber in a lush forest. They walked with only that sound until he filled the void. "Ye need a maid. We'll see to one while we are in the village."

Panic welled inside her. "I told ye before, I dinnae want one."

"My wife will be properly fitted into her gowns, and yer hair is a mess." She had the urge to try to fix her hair, but her hand was frozen. Argh, she would not let his words hurt her.

Halting again, she enunciated the words as clearly as she could as she said, "I dinnae want a maid. I will learn how to do it myself if it offends ye so." She pulled her wayward curls back, tying the unruly locks into a knot at the top of her head. She stomped ahead, up the path and toward the village where she hoped there wouldn't be another thing said about the issue.

. . .

Despite her reluctance, his wife would have a maid. Normally, Grant would honor a lass's wishes, but with her wind-tossed hair and loosened clothing, his thoughts kept turning to nights sequestered under their covers.

All he'd been able to think about as he'd fallen asleep was tasting her lips and discovering if she would gently inhale him again. The idea that she'd been so affected by their simple kiss caused an ache in his cock. Perhaps he'd been too long without a woman's touch, but he wanted to explore every inch of her sleek form. *Damn*, if he were honest, he'd been infatuated with her the first moment he'd seen her.

He had needed a new wife, but had not wanted *this* lass, one who would go to war with Argyll himself if given the chance. The first time she'd caught his eyes, she'd been covered in dirt and wearing men's clothing in the heat of a battle. She'd looked like an avenging angel then, but he'd certainly not expected her to look like a conquering goddess of mythology or a wanton temptress no matter the time of day.

Her disheveled garments made him think of bed play. He didn't want to be having these thoughts, so she had to be dressed properly or he might be tempted to plunder her spoils and forget himself before he fully trusted her.

He'd pulled her gown together and tightened the laces, but the desire to loosen the bindings farther and take her to the hidden cave down the shore where they could be alone had been all too real and too sudden to examine.

Thankfully, she had asked about Lyall, bringing him back to his senses and reminding him not of the complacent wife who had been of an arranged marriage, but of her brother, his friend, the one who now lay cold in the ground. The man he'd not been able to protect because Isobel had distracted him from the battle. She was a seasoned killer and not a woman to underestimate.

Maybe it had been the sadness that had crept into her brown gaze as her family deserted her to a man who despised her which had given him some misplaced sympathy for the lass. But, *damn*, she didn't have the right to even know Lyall's name.

As they approached the stables at the top of the hill, she spoke. "Will I be allowed the use of a horse?"

"Aye. Despite what ye believe, ye arenae a prisoner here. I will provide ye with yer own."

"There is nae need. I will only use one occasionally. I dinnae mind sharing."

He felt his brow quirk. Who only wanted to *borrow* a horse? How could a person rely on a steed or it have faith in you without a bond formed by familiarity?

Once they reached the stables, he had his horse and one belonging to his cousin, Skye, brought around. The lass had moved back to Cameron lands, and her mount needed some attention; maybe the mare and Isobel would suit until he could find her a horse of her own.

As they trotted down the tree-lined path to the village, he wondered how he would feel about his wife if he'd not come upon her on that fateful day and didn't know about her association with the Resistance.

"Why do ye fight?"

"How can I no' when my family will be forced to accept the Covenanters' wishes?" Her flippant response disturbed him.

"There are other men to fight this battle. What if we can win the war with peace?"

"And do ye believe that can happen?" she scoffed.

"There is a chance."

She laughed and anger crept in, but he tamped it down. Sun peeked through the thick foliage canopy and lit her light brown hair, almost giving it a golden glow.

"We must always choose peace if we have the option." He had men to protect and throwing them into battle without proper thought was reckless.

She mumbled something under her breath as she stared straight ahead.

"What?"

"Then ye are a fool," she repeated, turning cold and

distant as her chin tilted up defiantly.

Fury roared in his chest. Did Isobel have no sense of self-preservation? Clenching his fists, he counted as he worked to control his breathing. "Dinnae ever call me that again, wife," he ordered, his voice booming and echoing through the trees and dense shrubbery they rode past.

She didn't apologize, but she did nod. Maybe Isobel possessed some intellect, and perhaps he even witnessed a little bit of remorse creep into her eyes.

He wouldn't believe she was right. He couldn't afford to let go of hope, but how was he to broker peace in a nation divided when he couldn't even find harmony with his wife?

"Yer hair has fallen down again." Damn if she didn't look like one of the fae come to Earth to wreak havoc on a man's desires. He fought the urge to extend his arm and twirl the tresses between his fingers to test its softness.

Shrugging, she smiled.

"A maid would help ye keep it in place." And possibly keep his mind from straying toward reaching out to touch her.

"A maid would poke me with pins and cause my head to hurt," her voice clipped.

"Is there nae subject we can talk about without arguing?"

"The weather," she said as they reached the edge of the village.

Maybe she would be onto something if the weather weren't so boring to talk about. He tried anyway. "What is yer perfect day, then?"

"I love storms. Not just a rain, but the kind that crashes around ye and makes ye aware of every second and that ye are alive." Her voice lightened.

Of course she would. "And what is wrong with a beautiful sunny day like we have now?" He breathed in the fresh air and glanced toward the nearly cloudless blue sky before guiding them to a post where they could secure the horses.

"It fools ye into believing that everything is right with the world, and that men can be trusted."

He dismounted and, without thinking, stepped over and took her by the waist to help her down. Her skirts brushed against him and he caught her exotic sent. He wanted to breathe it in until he knew it, until he could put a name to the fragrance of Isobel. He pulled her nearer than intended, her body so close to his that he could feel her warmth.

As he set his wife on her feet they both froze. They stood locked together, face to face, her warm gaze calling to him. His fingers still clutched her trim middle. They tingled. And he wanted to kiss her. Swallowing, he dropped his arms and put some distance between them.

Then he remembered her words. "How do ye no' have any belief that some men can be good?" he questioned.

"They aren't." She shook her head.

"'Tis foolish to judge a man before ye ken him." He turned to tether their mounts and she started walking.

"I thought ye wanted to stop arguing," she said when he came up beside her.

Isobel tilted her head away. Maybe he shouldn't have been so harsh, but what had irritated him was that they couldn't even agree on the weather and she had no faith in men. Rain had its merits, but storms always reminded Grant of the day his uncle died. His father's youngest brother had only been three years older than Grant and they'd grown up as if they had been siblings. And if the man had had more faith in others and not rushed into battle, he might still be alive.

After hours of exploring the village and introducing his bride to his people, they settled in at one of the taverns for an afternoon meal.

After the server brought them trenchers filled with roasted meat, potatoes, and sugared carrots, he asked, "What will ye miss most about yer home?"

Isobel remained silent, but he could see her turning the question over in her head. He expected her to come back with something like her best friend or her brothers or her bed, but she surprised him and maybe herself as well when she replied, "I dinnae ken."

"Is there nothing?"

"What would ye miss if ye were pawned off by yer family to another?" Bitterness entered her tone.

"'Tis easy. My family, my horse, the mist, and the salty smell of the air on the water that protects us from enemies."

She perked up and smiled. "My sword and my daggers. That is what I miss."

Shaking his head, he remembered the disarmingly bonny lass in front of him was actually the fierce battle-hardened warrior he'd first met with blood on her blade. *If she hadn't been there.* He pushed the image from his head and took a bite of the potatoes, concentrating on the buttery taste and forcing his thoughts somewhere else. He wanted to find common ground with his wife, but he didn't know where to start.

Isobel looked dejected after working so hard for an answer, but it had soured his mood and quite possibly was the worst thing she could have said. They ate the rest of the meal in silence, then he stood. "Wait here. I'll be right back."

Strolling over to the tavern owner he'd known his whole life, he pulled the man aside. "Did I hear one of yer daughters is qualified to be a lady's maid?"

"Aye. Annis has had some training."

"My wife needs a maid. Would she be interested?" He spared a glance back to the table to assure himself Isobel couldn't hear him and that she hadn't fled.

"Aye, she would." The man's head bobbed and a large smile presented itself.

"Then send her to Cairntay to start tomorrow."

"Will yer wife no' want to meet her first?" The man seemed confused.

"Nae, she needs someone now, and I know she'll love Annis." Grant smiled back at the tavern keeper.

"She will be there tomorrow early, then."

Pleased, he returned to the table to collect Isobel. After they gathered the horses, they headed back toward Cairntay. About halfway there, his wife stopped and he turned to see she was climbing from the mare's back. What was the crazy lass doing now?

He dismounted while she was tying off the horse to a nearby tree. Once it was secured to the solid, low-hanging branch of an oak, she tiptoed toward the small, fast-flowing creek that filled the air with sounds of soft running water and ran parallel to the path. Following her gaze, he noticed a small roughhewn bag lying haphazardly on the bank as if someone had attempted to toss it in the water. It was secured at one end with a length of rope.

A little squeal came from the bag, then another. Isobel rushed straight for the bag as if her life depended on it. After untying the rope, his wife opened the bag, and a tiny gray-and-white head with ears that flopped down and big rounded eyes popped up.

She sank to the ground, pulling the bag and creature closer to her, heedless of the dirt. The wee creature clawed the rest of the way out of the bag, climbing into his wife's lap and rubbing its head against her hand as it complained loudly.

"Who would do such a thing?" she said to herself more than to him.

Moving closer, he glanced down at the small cat making itself at home in Isobel's skirts. "It appears to like ye." *Trusting little creature*, he thought, but then let his gaze rise to his wife's, which was fixated on the wee little thing with kindness.

She glanced up at him and he could see her eyes had grown wide. She shook her head. "Nae, it cannae. We will find it a home." Isobel stroked the kitten's cheek and then its back. "How could someone toss a defenseless animal into the water?" He heard compassion in Isobel's voice and leaned in closer, almost wanting to be near her. Almost wanting her to feel that way about him.

"I find it hard to understand others, sometimes. The creature is lucky the person missed the water and also fortunate ye found it."

"What do we do with it?" After scooping it into her hands, she held the kitten up and pushed it toward him, but he didn't move to claim it.

"'Tis up to ye. I think it wants to stay with ye."

"I cannae care for a pet." Was that panic in her typically fearless gaze? She pulled the wee thing back into her lap, but looked away from it.

"Why?"

Her mouth fell open but she didn't answer. Then he remembered what Isobel's brother, Ross, had said about her pushing people away. Perhaps the creature would be good for her.

The kitten crawled over her hand and climbed up her gown to snuggle into Isobel's neck. The bewildered expression on her face softened her somehow, made her look vulnerable and reachable, like a lost child.

Could it be that his wife actually had a nurturing side?

Chapter Four

The wee kitten was soft as it burrowed into the space between her neck and her hair, tickling Isobel's sensitive skin. A small giggle escaped her as it started making noises akin to the men in the Royalist Resistance camp who snored, except this noise was pleasant to the ears and pleasing to the senses as the little vibrations massaged her flesh. She pulled the creature down, holding it out by the scruff of its neck as she'd seen someone else do once.

"How do we find it a home?" Holding it toward her husband once again, she tried to get him to take it, but he looked at her as if she'd lost her mind, or as if he wanted to laugh at her.

"Ye will have to carry it as ye ride."

Panic welled inside her. She couldn't carry it, but she couldn't leave it here. It might not survive in these dense woods. Deer tracks littered the bank and the area probably harbored many dangers, like wildcats and foxes.

"I dinnae ken how to hold a cat." She drew it into her lap, where it proceeded to climb back up to her neck.

"Then 'tis time ye learned." Grant held out a hand to help her from the ground. She took it, noticing how solid and reassuring it felt, and she realized it was the first time they had really connected. Unbidden, her gaze fell to his lips; they were full and a pleasant shade of rose. *Hell*, she wanted to kiss him again. She shook the thought from her mind.

"Why can't ye take it?"

"Because it likes ye."

Nae, it couldn't like her. What was she to do with a pet? It would only get in her way, but the big amber-colored eyes pleaded for help. Swallowing, she decided to carry it back, but she would be finding it a home as soon as possible.

"Here." She held it out for him to take as she climbed onto the mare. He cradled the kitten and murmured some words to the creature, but she couldn't make them out.

He held it up to her, and she shook her head. "Why don't ye keep it? Ye seem to ken what yer doing with it."

"Ye saved it."

Frowning, she sighed and held out her hands. She would argue, but he still had to climb onto his horse. The only other option was leaving it, but how would it survive?

"And 'tis fun to see ye no' in control of something." Those bonny blue eyes of his lit with mirth as he smiled up at her.

Was he making fun of her? He wanted to see her flustered. Sitting up straighter, she pretended she knew what she was doing. She chose not to give his remarks or the smirk on his face any credence. Instead, she held the wee thing in one arm and drove the horse on with the other.

Thankfully, the ride back to Cairntay was short, because the little thing kept digging its claws into her gown and attempting to climb into her hair. She'd almost dropped it on a couple of occasions.

After stabling the horses, she held it out to him, but a grin spread across his face as he crossed his arms and shook his head. He was amused by her discomfort and what made it worse was that she was finding she enjoyed seeing a smile on his face.

"What does it eat?" she asked.

"Have ye never had a pet before?"

"Nae, and I dinnae want one."

"Looks like ye have nae choice. They like cream and meat. Come," he said as they walked through the empty yard at the back of Cairntay. He led her to a little building half buried in the ground near the castle walls. After taking the steps down, Grant lifted the latch and pushed open the door, hooking it on something to keep it ajar.

"The larder?" she asked as they walked in.

"Aye. We'll find something in here for it."

"I cannae see a thing." The only light came from behind them and the clouds blotted out most of the sun's rays.

"Give me a moment." And just a few breaths later, Grant had a candle lit.

Shelves were piled high with provisions, but she had no idea what she was looking for. After she set the creature down and lost its warmth, she noticed the room had a chill to it, just like the larder back home. The kitten must have missed their connection as well, because it started climbing up her skirts, claws pulling at the material.

Gasping, she backed away, bumping into the door and loosening the latch when she hit her head on a shelf. "Ouch."

"Nae," Grant called out and lunged for the door, but in his haste, he pushed it farther along on its course. He crashed into the frame and the walls seemed to shudder with the force. The sound of banging metal gave her a sickening dread in the pit of her stomach.

Rubbing her head, she blinked, trying to adjust to only the candlelight in the room. The kitten had found her, its claws clinging her skirts. "Ah." She pulled the creature free.

She wouldn't be surprised if the new gown had tears in it from the animal's vicious talons.

Banging on the door, Grant yelled, "In here." He continued for several moments before giving in and turning his frustration on her. "It appears we are stuck for now."

"'Tis nae my fault."

"Ye should have been more careful. Ye seem to be good at doing things without thinking."

"Are ye referring to this or something else? I can assure ye I never do anything without thought." How dare he blame her for this.

"Then that makes some of yer decisions even worse." He seemed to loom over her in the small space, the light shining on him as she backed a step. *Hell*, she was never afraid of anyone, and she was not going to let her husband have the advantage.

"If anyone is to blame, 'tis ye. I told ye I dinnae ken anything about these creatures. Ye should have taken it." Peeling it from her arms again, she held it out to him. But this time the cat twisted, clawing at her, trying to hang on.

"Ouch." The kitten fell, landing on its paws and scrambling into the dark. Turning away from her husband, she held her arm toward the candle to inspect the damage. Three lines had formed on her skin, small traces of red seeping through them. Then she felt her husband's presence beside her. He reached down and took her arm.

"Are ye all right?"

"I will be." She breathed in as his woodsy scent invaded her.

His fingers traced the sensitive skin around the injury, and strange tingles pulsed out from the connection. Her chest tightened because, heaven help her, she wanted to kiss him. She attempted to retreat, and although his grip was gentle it was firm. Instead of pulling free, she managed to draw his solid body into hers.

Glancing up into his eyes, she wasn't sure if they had darkened or if it was just the room, but he didn't release her. She swallowed. His free hand coiled around her waist, gently cradling her to him. A foreign feeling erupted somewhere inside her and instead of pushing him away, she held still to examine it.

The hand holding her injured arm slid up past her shoulder, over her neck, and fingers delved into her hair as her body decided not to obey her command to retreat. His hand threaded its way into her scalp then removed the few pins she'd been able to secure there.

She found her feet moving backward as he guided her into the closed door. Tugging gently at her loosened strands of hair, he tilted her face up toward his. The next thing she knew, his lips were crashing down on hers and sweeping her into something new, something she had never wanted before that made her insides ignite with unexplored desires.

Oh, *hell*, she liked it.

· · ·

Grant wasn't sure what he was doing, but he couldn't stop. Her skin was surprisingly soft beneath his rough hands. And the way she trembled at his touch when her gaze focused on him had every muscle in his body tightening. She looked so bonny in the candlelight. Her lips parted in what appeared to be an invitation. Isobel's attention pulled him in, making him want to see if she put as much effort into the mating between a man and a woman as she did into fighting.

He would need an heir one day; why should he deny himself her body because he didn't approve of her past actions? She was his wife, after all. *His*. And judging by the way she gasped into his mouth as his tongue delved in between her parted lips, she was completely his. Despite all the time she'd spent pretending to be a man and with men, she'd never kissed one. How was that even possible?

His wife had secrets, and he suddenly found himself wanting to know more. How was it no man had ever touched her? How would it feel to claim her body as his own, and why had he let his anger stop him last night?

Tentatively, her tongue reached out, dancing with his, sending him into a spiraling mix of confusion and need mingled with frustration at himself that despite who she was, he wanted her. A violent explosion of emotions found him backing her into the hard surface of the door and covering her body with his. She gasped into his mouth and he slowed as he was reminded of her innocence, something easily overlooked by her experience on the battlefield. The contradiction perplexed him, drawing him in; he eased, letting the hand around her waist drop to gently caress her ass and pull her taut with the throbbing pain between his legs.

Letting his mouth stray from hers, he moved to her neck and nibbled on the soft flesh as a whiff of her exotic scent cascaded through his senses and spurred him on. As he sucked on the sensitive skin, she moaned and arched into him. Her hands clasped on to his hips as if he were driving her down a perilous road with nothing but him to hold on to. He was rewarded with a soft, pleading whimper. She might fight like a man, but she was all woman underneath.

A sudden push at her back jarred them. He let his mouth drop from her neck. Another push. Stepping aside, he hid her behind his back as the door swung in to reveal one of the kitchen servants.

"Excuse us," he said as the newcomer reddened. "We were locked in trying to find something for the cat." Why was he trying to explain? He could take his wife anywhere he wanted, but she deserved better than him thrusting into her in the larder in the middle of the day.

Tiny claws scratched at his legs as the forgotten kitten made its presence known. "Ah, there's the wee thing." After picking up the kitten, he held it out for the servant to see, as if he should offer an explanation for assaulting his wife in a most inappropriate place.

The man just smiled. "I'll be back in a few minutes. I forgot something." The door almost closed behind him, but Grant reached out and caught it.

"Here." His voice was harsh as he rounded on Isobel and gave her the cat. How had he forgotten himself yet again around her? Just as he had the day Tomas had died.

The sun had reemerged and shone into the space where they were standing. He realized he'd left a mark on her neck. He'd never done that to a woman before, but he'd never had a woman so wantonly give in to his attentions. Her lips were swollen and a deeper shade of red, and her hair was mussed as if they'd spent hours alone together, not the few moments it had taken him to come completely unhinged. And, oblivious to their surroundings.

Angered at himself that he'd lost control and nearly taken her with the food storages, he passed her the kitten. "Feed it."

He lost his senses when he was near Isobel and that led to trouble. He walked a short distance away to wait for her as he thought about his dead friend and stifled the desire to truly make Isobel his wife.

• • •

Hours later, he found himself sitting at the table for the evening meal when the object of his affliction walked in with his mother. She wore the same dress, but she'd brushed her hair and left it to fall loose around her shoulders and cascade to her waist, where it slid back and forth over her curves. He'd spent the afternoon trying to forget how those curves felt, but it had been no use.

As she sat a few spaces down from him, his eyes strayed toward her. She was fidgeting with her hair, pulling it to the front and covering her neck. He grinned. She was trying to conceal the mark he'd left on her. He found himself wanting to see it, wanting to show that he had claimed her like no man ever had.

His father drew his attention back with, "Are ye and yer wife getting along?"

"As well as we can."

"She was with yer mother late this afternoon. I believe they toured the castle when ye returned from the village. Where were ye?"

"In the lists." He probably should have been the one to show Isobel her new home, but he'd needed exertions to ease his mind after he'd lost himself in her embrace. After their kiss, he promptly deposited her in the great room with his mother and hurried back outside.

"Ah, so it's going that well, huh." Laughter escaped his father's lips. He leaned in, winking. "Ye should spend that energy bedding yer wife. Ye have to continue on our legacy."

Angered by his father's meddling, his voice rose, but he didn't care. "Ye ken she is responsible for Tomas's death?"

The laird's eyes darkened.

"Do ye think Lyall would want her in our bed? She'd probably demand justice." He regretted the words as soon as they'd left his lips, because they weren't true. Lyall would have liked Isobel and she would be happy he had found a wife who matched his spirit.

His father shook his head as if warning him something was wrong, but it was too late. The hall had gone quiet and every eye was on Grant, or actually, directly behind him. Turning, he saw Isobel, face pale and eyes the size of saucers, staring down at her plate as if she were a deer about to be slaughtered.

Her humiliation seemed to change to anger as she took in all the unfamiliar faces, their sympathy aimed at her. He sank down into his chair, ashamed he'd embarrassed Isobel in front of half the clan. He typically kept his temper in check, because as heir to the chief, he would one day need the respect of the clan.

But everything about this lass drove him to madness. It was his only excuse. Straightening her shoulders, she turned her back to him and his mother glared over Isobel's shoulder, promising a solid set down when she was able to get him cornered.

Chapter Five

After slamming the door, Isobel stomped into the chamber she now shared with Grant. Had the arse intentionally accused her of murder in front of his whole clan? Why had he not talked to her about it? And why did he think her capable of murdering an innocent man?

Contemplating escape again, she strode over to the window and looked out over the choppy waters being beaten by high winds and a storm that had moved in this afternoon. After their kiss.

She'd never allowed a man to touch her before. Despite how pleasurable it had been, she now regretted not pushing Grant away. *Och*, but the gentle way he'd held her had sent tingles through her arm and apparently shut down her good sense.

Her husband didn't want her here and she didn't want to be here. If she could convince her family that he'd rejected her, maybe they would let her come home.

Hell, maybe he'd toss her out anyway. She didn't think her husband capable of murder. Still, she'd been able to sneak a dirk tonight and would hide it under the bedside table.

The kitten pounced from under the bed, attacking the hem of her skirts. Argh, after trying unsuccessfully all afternoon to find a home for it, she'd left it in the kitchens. How had it found its way up here?

"Stop it." She brought the wee thing up to her cheek. "Ye belong here nae more than I do. At least ye can get away." She opened the door, then tried to set it outside, but it clung to her gown as if sensing the loneliness of the dark, quiet hall. "Och, I guess ye can stay tonight, but tomorrow ye must go. I am not capable of taking care of ye."

So he had been married before and considered this his first wife's bed. Why would a woman she'd never met think her such a horrid person? Her gaze shifted to the other furniture in the room. None of this belonged to her, and her husband didn't want her here.

Rummaging through a cabinet, she found blankets and laid a couple down on the hard wooden floor in the opposite corner of the room then inspected her work. It would do—it wouldn't be much different from the ground on her nights with the Resistance.

She moved over to the trunks she hadn't bothered to unpack and riffled through for a clean shift. She smiled at the small box packed inside, and opening it, found several vials that had been secured within the velvet lining. At least her family had sent her something from home.

She opened one and pulled it up to her nose to inhale the jasmine oil. It had been her childhood maid's favorite and always reminded her of happy times. A finger to the top of the container, she tilted it then caught a drop and placed one behind each ear. When she'd told Grant she wouldn't miss anything from home, she'd forgotten about this scent.

The ritual calmed her and gave renewed purpose to her thoughts. She had a duty to protect those she cared for, and she would find a way to do it again.

She replaced the stopper then stood, undressed, and put on the shift. When she sank onto the pallet on the floor, the kitten jumped from the bed. It curled up next to her as she closed her eyes and wondered how to ask her husband if he would let her have a separate room, or better yet, let her leave.

• • •

"Ye will take her with ye," The MacDonald laird instructed after dinner when they'd reached his study.

Grant groaned as his father glared at him from behind the big oak desk. He'd hoped to sneak outside for a bit of fresh air before going up to face his wife, but his father insisted on speaking with him in private.

"Why can she no' stay here? I dinnae want her with me." His father had to know she would not be the best companion on a journey trying to secure peace in the Highlands.

"'Tis the point. Ye embarrassed yer new bride in front of the whole clan. If it gets back to the MacLeans that ye've left her before a week is out and arenae treating her well…" His father left the rest unsaid. "Besides, 'twas an awful thing to do to someone who is an outsider and hasnae had a chance to prove herself."

"She's a bloodthirsty savage. I saw her run after a man who had just sliced into her arm."

"Have ye even given her a chance to explain what happened?"

"Nae, I saw it with my own eyes." Grant fisted his hands.

"She deserves the opportunity to explain, and she deserves a husband who will give her that chance. She's only been here a day and ye've already shunned her in front of everyone. If ye are going to lead the clan one day, ye will need heirs and ye will need to put on a unified front."

"I dinnae think we want her to prove what she is capable of." That earned a snort from his father.

"If ye are set on trying to broker peace, ye will take her. It will give ye two the opportunity to ken each other and prove to the clan ye can work together when necessary."

For the first time ever, Grant dreaded the obligation to his clan, but his father was correct. He did need to find common ground with Isobel. He wanted to see past her rugged exterior, and perhaps the forced closeness on this trip would be better than avoiding her. He'd already discovered she had a nurturing side with the cat, even though she attempted to hide it.

"Besides, the other Highland lairds are all sending representatives, and it is important to show them that we have made this treaty with the MacLeans," his father continued.

He had to admit dressing Isobel like a lady and putting her in the role of a dutiful wife would alleviate any suspicion thrown her way. He'd caught her trailing her finger reverently across the silk of her gown yesterday. Perhaps the garments would grow on her. He would just have to keep weapons out of her hands.

"Ye should be ready to leave by the end of the week. And ye'll travel faster if ye take a smaller party. Be vigilant, though. Argyll's men are everywhere."

"Aye, I ken the dangers." Grant swallowed.

With a nod, he turned and strolled from the room, making his way to the kitchen instead of the chamber where his wife would be. There, in the empty room, he poured himself a glass of whisky and fought the emotions swirling inside.

He tried to push away the memory of the kiss they had shared this afternoon. The contradiction that was Isobel. Was she an innocent like her kiss and body had proclaimed, or was she a killer like his eyes had seen?

His groin tightened as he remembered the taste of her.

But how could he be so disloyal to his first wife, sleeping with the woman who had been the cause of her brother's death? Claiming his husbandly rights would betray the memory of his friend.

But he also had a duty to his clan. He poured one more dram, downed it, and made his way up to the bed where his new wife would be.

When he pushed open the door, he was surprised to see she had left a candle burning for him on the nightstand. In the light of it, he plodded over to the bed, but she wasn't there. Panic hit him first, worry that something had happened to her. Then it struck him that she may have had the audacity to try to leave Skye. But before he rushed out to look for her, he saw a bundle in the far end of the room.

He picked up the candle and walked over to make sure she was there. She looked peaceful, her hair spread behind her like wings that might carry her away. His gaze drifted down to the darkened circle on her neck, the one he'd put there.

A shot of desire surged in him and he froze then shook his head at the little gray lump by Isobel's belly. The wee kitten was curled up next to her, and the lass actually looked innocent and harmless.

Dreading tomorrow and the rest of his nights spent tied to this woman, he ground his teeth. *Damn*, he might not like her, but she was his wife and he wouldn't have her sleep on the floor like a dog. He strolled back to the bed and put down the candle then pulled back the covers enough so she would fit. Satisfied, he gathered her and the small creature up in his arms and carried them back to the bed.

Undressing, he blew out the candle and crawled under the covers. The scent that was only Isobel reached his nose and made him want to pull her near so he could inhale her sweetness. But doing so would reawaken his desire to plunge into her, so he turned his back and tried to sleep.

He tossed all night, one minute wanting Isobel, the next wanting to heave her into the sea. How was he to survive this marriage with his sanity intact?

Chapter Six

Isobel felt a tiny jolt near her head and something nudging her cheek just before a wet, scratchy tongue scraped across her jaw. The wee creature apparently needed some kind of attention. Then she found her husband next to her asleep, more relaxed than she'd ever seen him.

It was a shame he wore that scowl all the time. Well that wasn't quite true; she'd spied him when he wasn't watching her and he was quite bonny when not looking in her direction. Unfortunately, he wanted nothing to do with her. So how had she gotten into the bed the woman he'd once loved wouldn't want her in?

Inching backward, she slid from the mattress. The kitten pounced onto the floor, following her and squealing so loudly the wee beast would probably wake Grant before she could escape the room. The less time she spent in that man's company the better. It was time to make a plan and where better to do that than the lists. Early morning sparring always brought clarity.

Scooping up the little ball of fur so it would hush, she

moved to the trunks she'd yet to unpack. She picked the lightest weight of the gowns she could find and quickly dressed then grabbed her slippers to put on in the hall.

Once out the door, she set the creature down and walked toward the back steps. They were wide, with just enough room for people to pass each other comfortably. The gray stones were level. Whoever had designed the castle had taken great care not only to give it strong turrets to defend its inhabitants, but to allow agreeable living conditions. The little kitten bounded after her. In the kitchens, she passed a lass preparing something for the morning meal. "Good morning."

The young woman blinked, likely surprised to see someone else up so early. "Good morning," she returned.

"Can I trouble ye by leaving this"—she pointed to the cat—"with ye for a bit. I cannae seem to get rid of it."

The girl laughed. "Aye, but ye will have to come back for it. Cook doesnae like cats in the kitchen."

"Do ye ken anyone who would want it? I cannae care for a pet."

"Nae, I dinnae."

"I'm Isobel."

"'Tis lovely to meet ye. I'm Jean."

"Could ye point me in the direction of the lists?"

"Aye, out that door, if ye look out to the left, ye will see the stables. 'Tis just on the other side."

"Thank ye."

Isobel went the opposite direction, back toward the great hall. Momentarily forgetting her mission, she studied the finery of the room, the lush tapestries woven with colorful threads of gold, red, and green. They depicted scenes of harvests and triumphs in battles, showing the history and majesty of Clan MacDonald. Wooden benches and tables filled the room and glowed golden in the early morning light streaming in through the tall clear-glazed windows. Grains of red flowed through their smooth surface. The solid structures seemed to be constructed from the trunks of the bonny oaks she'd seen on their journey into the village yesterday.

She pulled her thoughts from the opulence of the room and scraped a chair across the floor, pulling it over to the wall. She reached up and grabbed one of the claymores that had been hung in either a display of vanity or for readiness should an enemy attack. It was a little heavier than her sword, but would give her good exercise.

Skirting back out of the hall and through the kitchens, she made her way out for some time to practice and think. The fresh air seeped into her limbs and brought a peace she'd not felt since being told she was here to become Grant MacDonald's bride.

Men were already at practice on the well-used fields carpeted with yellowing, flattened grass and patches of exposed chestnut earth. Good. Her new clan would have at least some men ready to safeguard the women and children should the need arise.

She found a spot some distance from them, where an imaginary opponent had been set up. Really, it was just a straw-stuffed post wearing clothing with ropes wound around to give it some stability. It would do nicely.

She pulled her skirts up and tied them off on both sides, well above the end of her shift. She would need the room to move about if she were to train in earnest today. The men were watching her, but she paid them no heed.

She lifted the sword and began thrashing at her mark. At first, it took on the appearance of Torsten Campbell, the bastard who threatened her identity and had gotten her into this mess.

It wasn't long ago when the Covenanters planned to attack a caravan of Macnabs, including one of her few friends, Kirstie Cameron, on their way to a meeting in Edinburgh. Isobel was determined to keep the lass safe and she hadn't realized they'd gone after a different group. One of MacDonalds and MacPhersons.

She was normally a spy and only fought in battles when someone she knew was in trouble or if Stew was going to be anywhere near the skirmish. She cared that there was an ongoing conflict between the clans' loyalties and religions, but she was there mostly to protect those she loved. Usually her brothers, because she rarely let herself get close to anyone else.

By the time she'd realized the Covenanters had attacked the wrong party, the Royalist Resistance had moved forward and she'd been caught in the fray. That was where she'd been distracted by the Highlander giving orders and striking down an attack against one of his own. He had hair the color of the darkest peat and wielded a sword with deadly precision.

He was a born leader, and it was obvious by the way the men around him flanked out in a fighting formation that he was in complete control and held their respect. For a moment, she'd wondered what it would be like to fight by his side and be under his protection, because the motley band of the Resistance couldn't be trusted. Although the men respected their leader, Alex, each member held their own agenda.

Then a tall Covenanter with reddish-brown hair had blocked her view and reminded her of the battle raging around them. Shock registered when she recognized Torsten Campbell.

"Isobel MacLean," the man had said with derision then a pleased grin spread across his face. "Argyll has been looking for a reason to bring yer clan to its knees. Imagine what he'll do when he discovers the notorious woman of the Resistance is ye."

She'd tightened her grip on her short sword, preparing to

fight—her family's well-being depended on it. If he walked away, she, her family, and her clan would be targets for the Covenanter leader. Raising her sword, she countered, "Ye willnae live to tell him."

The man thrust with his sword, connecting with hers and trying to knock it free from her hands, but she held, despite the massive size of the brute. Spinning, she came back around swinging, but he blocked her progress. "I will live, and what do ye think he will do to ye when I bring ye to him alive?"

She swung around low, aiming for his legs, but he angled his bigger sword just in time to deflect yet another blow. Laughing, he pushed back and she stumbled.

"Of course I'll have some fun with ye before I deliver ye to the earl." His eyes had raked down to her chest.

Now knowing he wanted her alive, her mind had churned as a plan developed. He was larger than most men and, despite her skill, she couldn't beat his brute force, so she would need to get him close enough to sink her dagger into him. That meant letting him believe she was helpless.

"When I bring ye to him, he'll finally give me the recognition I deserve," Torsten had jeered.

"I willnae be going anywhere with ye."

"Ye will, lass. Ye are the key to what I've always wanted."

"And what is that?" She held her sword out in front of her, preparing to attack.

"My cousin's respect. When he sees what I've brought him, he'll make me a general."

This time when Campbell lunged, she let him knock the sword from her hand, but she'd misjudged his momentum and the point of his blade sliced into her shoulder. It wasn't a deep cut, but blood spilled from the wound, coating her shirt as the man moved in to grab her other arm. She almost had her hand on her blade, readying to sink it into his unsuspecting gut, when the commanding Highlander leaped forward and knocked the man backward, freeing her from his grasp and thwarting her opportunity to take him down.

The leader regained his control, lifting a claymore and moving into a battle stance between she and her mark. The Campbell steadied his footing then stood to face off with the Highlander.

A call came for retreat. Torsten Campbell turned and ran. She started after him but the Highlander grabbed her arm and twisted her around. "'Tis no' safe, lass. He'll kill ye."

"I had it in hand."

She'd tried to pull free, but his grip was firm, determined. His regard turned to her crimson shirt. "We need to get ye to a healer."

She didn't have time for this. "I have to kill him," she blurted as she tried to ignore the striking blue of the man's eyes.

His sapphire gaze had darkened, pinning her, and his rough voice ordered, "Stand down."

"Ye have nae right to order me about."

He started to say more, but his attention was drawn to something behind her. His grip tightened for a moment and his glare clouded, then he let go of her and she ran after the Campbell, but he was gone.

Returning her focus to the list and the present, she imagined her target was now her husband, the man who had stopped her from protecting her family and stolen the rest of her life. "I dinnae want to be wed to ye, either," she continued and thrust at the mark.

"I dinnae belong here." She thrust again.

"Ye let him get away." The heat of her efforts flushed her, but she continued to pound out her frustration.

"I have to go find him."

Now it was her own face she saw.

"Ye failed again. They will be hurt because of ye."

Wetness trailed down her cheek.

"Ye canne let him get to them."

"'Tis all yer fault." Winded, she swung so hard when she struck this time, the force reverberated back into her arms, stinging her elbows and shoulders.

"Wife." A commanding voice intruded, and she pivoted, then let the sword dangle to her side as she blinked to bring Grant into focus.

· · ·

Sword in hand, Isobel spun around to face Grant as if an enemy were about to attack. It was like she'd been in a battle for her life and not merely sparring with the straw man she'd hacked to pieces.

"What the hell do ye think yer doing?"

Sweat beaded on her brow. She blinked as her chest rose and fell with heavy breaths, drawing his eyes down to the gown haphazardly laced and showing more of her shift than it should. Gaze drifting lower, he studied the way she'd tied her skirts up on the sides. The bloodthirsty wench couldn't go two days without looking for a victim.

Something odd caught his attention—a tear trailed down her face, not sweat from exertion. He wanted to move closer, to comfort her, but then he remembered how she'd rejected his offer of help when she'd been injured in the skirmish.

Looking away from the imagined display of emotion, he studied the sword she held. "Where did ye get that?"

"Are ye going to take it from me?" Her shoulders stiffened and her chin tilted up.

"Aye. Where?"

She rolled her eyes and his temper spiked, but he kept it in check until he could get the weapon from her hands.

"Ye have them lying about all over the place." She

shrugged and smirked as if he and his clan were crazy. He couldn't fathom what she was talking about until she continued, "The hall. They are on the walls."

He groaned. Perhaps she was correct, but it didn't seem plausible to remove them all because of one woman. He'd have to think on it some more—she didn't strike him as foolish, only reckless.

"Ye ken we have wooden swords for practice?" Not that he wanted her using anything.

"And if I had asked for one, ye would have given it?"

He shook his head.

"'Tis what I thought," she muttered and cast an angry glare his way.

"Come. We have things to discuss."

She turned toward the straw man as if she wanted one more go at it then slowly pivoted back and moved toward him. When she approached, he held out his hand. She extended the hilt of the sword toward him and let him take it without argument. She must be exhausted; he'd watched her for a good five minutes of nonstop thrusts before he'd interrupted her.

"Dinnae put me in that bed again." She met his gaze with eyes so dark and cold he imagined her slicing through him with the blade, but then he saw the real emotion behind her argument—she was hurt and he couldn't blame her after the words he'd blurted out the evening before. Maybe she wasn't all warrior. Maybe there was a heart beneath. A stab of guilt shot through him.

Still, he'd be dammed if he let her sleep on the floor. "Ye are my wife, and ye will sleep in my bed."

"Ye dinnae truly want me there."

He couldn't respond, because he wasn't sure what he wanted. He didn't want to want her, but he did. Even as he'd rushed out to the lists after his father's guard told him what she was doing, he'd stopped, mesmerized by her grace and control with the weapon. Her hair was tied back, but coming loose from whatever she'd secured it with, and her reddened cheeks gave her the appearance of a woman who had been thoroughly bedded. Even the rise and fall of her breasts as she fought to control her breathing had stirred in him the desire to take her back up to bed and claim his husbandly rights.

He didn't have to love his wife to want her. Just admitting that to himself opened up the possibility he could still get some enjoyment out of this arrangement. He did have to provide an heir, and maybe she would eventually thaw—she had when he'd kissed her before.

He remembered the tear. Knowing there must be some underlying reason, he asked her again, "Why do ye fight?"

"I have nae choice." A far-off look claimed her gaze, and he found himself wanting to turn her toward him and reassure her, but he kept his hands and the sword at his side. Instead, he studied the lass who was forcing him to face a range of emotions. Ones that made him feel as if he were bathing in the sun on a warm day then dipping into a cold loch, just to get out and be warmed again.

"Aye, ye do. Ye are safe here on MacDonald lands."

"Women are never safe." Her hands had fisted into her skirts. Isobel picked up the pace.

"Ye have a choice. I willnae let anything happen to ye." And he meant it. If anyone had the right to throttle her it would be him, not that he would ever lay a hand on her; she just drove him mad with her draw-yer-sword-first-find-the-truth-after attitude.

She nodded, but her evasive gaze told him she didn't believe him.

"Ye must let me go after Torsten Campbell."

He shook his head. There was no way he'd let her near

that man again. Seeing the arse's sword slice across Isobel's arm during the skirmish had made his heart skip a beat. What would happen if he saw some danger threaten her now that she was his wife?

"He kens who I am. If he finds me here, he will bring Argyll's forces with him and I dinnae wish that for ye or yer people."

"Our people." The sooner she thought of herself as one of them, the better.

"We must find him before he can tell the earl."

"Yer time for fighting is over. I'll deal with the Campbell man." Her lips pinched together, but he had a solution to the problem he was hopeful would work.

"He is nae a reasonable man and is faithful to his clan. There can be nae truce with him."

"There may still be an option that includes peace."

"Then ye are delusional."

His jaw ticked at her response as his hands clenched and unclenched at his side. Taking a deep breath, he calmed himself. "Is it wrong to hope for peace?"

"Nae. The error is to think ye will find it." This time she didn't sound judgmental; it was sadness he heard in her voice.

"Ye are mistaken. 'Tis reckless to risk others when ye are responsible for their well-being. I have people to look after and like it or no' ye are now one of them." They were back at the castle, and he held his free hand out for her to enter first. "To the hall. We shall break our fast first, then I have someone I want ye to meet."

Following her into the castle, he braced himself for the argument he knew was coming.

Chapter Seven

Isobel came to a halt in the hall and held out her hand. "Give me the sword and I'll put it away."

She nodded toward the empty space on the wall where a chair had been positioned so she could reach. Trusting her, he held out the hilt. She took it and smiled then walked over to the chair and climbed on. Grant noticed her strong calves, which were exposed by the way she'd tied her dress.

Murmurs reached his ears and he glanced around to see the room full of men also examining his wife's lack of decency. As she rose to insert the sword into the holder, her skirts lifted, almost exposing the backs of her knees. Then, she was climbing down again. He held out a hand and she took it, looking quite pleased. His gaze was drawn to the spot on her neck still purple from his attentions yesterday and then farther still to the gown that was so loose it looked as if someone had been trying to remove it.

It should have been him.

A surge of desire shot through him as he remembered the taste of her, the feel of her lean body smashed against his.

He shouldn't want this woman, but damn him, he did, and he didn't want others to see what she was so willingly putting on display. Something had to be done about her attire, and he hoped Annis had arrived.

"Change of plans." Drawing her through the door, he kept his hand on hers and guided her up the steps to their room.

"I am hungry. What are we doing?"

"Aye. I'm hungry too," he ground out, fighting his body's response to her nearness as they'd been pushed together on the narrow set of steps.

He opened the door, pulled his wife into their room, and shut it all in one fluid movement. When he had her alone, he swirled her around in front of him and as his breath became shallow, he moved into her.

She gasped as he latched onto her other hand and pinned both of them on either side of her. She didn't fight him as she did with her words; it was as if her body, too, had a primal reaction to him, uncontrollable and clambering to be obeyed. Her plump breasts rose and fell beneath her shift, and he groaned at the thought of tasting one of them.

"W-What?" Isobel stuttered, but her gaze said she knew exactly what he was thinking and wanting. Dipping his head, he was just moving in to take her mouth when a knock sounded at the door.

Stopping mid-descent, he prayed for the person to go away, to leave him with this wife who vexed him to no end. He wished to give in to what he'd been suppressing. Now that he acknowledged he didn't have to like her to perform his husbandly duty and enjoy her body, he wanted to delve into her and sate the need that had claimed him once he'd tasted her in the larder.

When no more rapping came, he continued, his lips landing on hers, needy and hungry. Her arms, which had tensed when he'd held them to her sides, relaxed and he felt her head tilt ever so slightly, allowing him better access as her body softened and her mouth opened to his.

Another knock jolted him, but he just stilled, not wanting to give up on the progress he'd made. Opening his eyes, he realized the door latch was not bolted. No. He'd not thought of that when they'd entered the room. *Damn*, he'd not been thinking about anything but claiming his wife.

"Grant." It was his mother's voice. Groaning, he reluctantly drew back, his gaze pinning on the bonny creature in front of him. With her eyes dazed and dilated, she didn't look like the killer he knew her to be, she looked like a woman in need of a good bedding. Despite the short kiss, her lips had deepened a shade and were swollen. They were still slightly parted as if waiting for him to continue. She looked like she could trust him and that made him want it to be true.

"Yes." His throaty reply was forced out as he tried to banish the desire coursing through him and the stray thought that had him wishing their union could become more.

"Annis is here. She said ye sent for her." Fenella's voice carried through the door.

"I did."

"Are ye ready for her? She is waiting in the kitchen. I'll send her up if ye are ready."

"Yes. Send her up." If he was quick, he could sate this lust that burned deep inside, but he couldn't do that to Isobel. He'd sensed yesterday she might be inexperienced. Even if he only wanted to claim his rights and forget about his wife, some small part of him spoke up and said it wouldn't be right. That she deserved more from him.

He had only been with a small handful of lasses, but none had made his loins ache this way. Maybe if Annis helped Isobel dress like a proper wife, he'd not feel this need so intensely. It was a desire like none he'd ever experienced.

Because, God help him, he didn't think he could resist Isobel on his own.

. . .

"Who is Annis?" Isobel asked as her husband released her hands and backed away. She'd been so enthralled by his touch she'd not thought to protest. A man had never taken such liberties with her and those who tried scurried away after she pulled her knife on them or Alex or one of his men stepped in to protect her.

This had been different. First of all, she didn't have a dirk on her and second, Grant made her feel something she'd never thought possible. *Hell*, they were married and she would need to experience lying with him at some point, but she'd never thought she might enjoy the act.

"She is yer new maid."

Stunned, she turned and moved deeper into the room, away from him, away from the memories that threatened to steal her breath.

Nae, nae, nae, he didn't. Her heart pumped harder trying to dislodge the dread that assailed her at the news. If anything could douse the flames heating her core, that did it. She rounded on him. "I dinnae want a maid."

"Ye will have one."

"Why?" She wanted to stamp her foot and act like a child. He could force her to his bed if he wanted, but he couldn't force her to accept a maid. This was where she drew the line.

"Ye can nae longer go around this keep dressed as if ye have just come from my bed."

"What?" He made no sense.

"Ye look as if we had been caught in the middle of some illicit tryst with the way yer dress falls off yer shoulder and ye hike it up to show off yer legs."

"There is nothing wrong with the way I dress. I dinnae need a maid."

"And yer hair. 'Tis time ye do something with it, because with it loose like this, it looks as if my fingers have been in it, mussing it while we..." He made a groaning noise and his eyes darkened and dilated.

"There is nothing wrong with my hair." Puffing out her chest, she stood taller, but he moved closer, becoming even bolder.

Wrapping his arm around her waist, he drew her into his hard frame. "As of now, ye have two choices."

She tilted her head up to his, listening to his warning.

"One, ye will accept her help and dress like a proper modest wife."

She shook her head, indicating she would not give.

After twirling her around, he pushed forward, toward the bed that had once belonged to his first wife. A few steps shy, he spun her to face him. "Or, two, ye will stay naked in this chamber ready for me to take ye whenever I want."

She was certain her mouth fell open. Had she ever been speechless before?

He inched closer, urging her back; she stopped just as her knees hit the mattress, halting their progress. Raising his hand, he let his fingers slide between her shift and the skin beneath. Gooseflesh rose on her arms. "Seeing ye like this makes me want to do things ye've probably never heard of, and if ye want to leave this room, ye will take the help."

Releasing her, he stormed from the room, slamming the door behind him as if she'd done something worthy of his wrath, then her gaze traveled down to the bed he'd once shared with another woman. A woman who would think her unworthy of him. *Hell*, she probably was, and although he'd awoken feelings in her that made her want to know more, she'd be damned if she would let him take her in that bed.

And he'd uttered something else hateful, too. He thought her responsible for some man's death. Tomas, he had said. The only men she'd killed had been a threat to Stew, the abandoned youth who had been taken in by Royalist Rebels. Grant was either mistaken, or he didn't know his friend well.

She moved to the chair and sat, waiting for the new maid to arrive. When a knock sounded at the door, she called out, "Enter."

The door creaked open slowly and as it did, the wee kitten came bounding in, running straight for her and clawing its way up her dress. Bending to help it, she pulled its talons from her skirts and nestled it close to her cheek. It started making that noise again, the one that made her want to snuggle up with it and go to sleep.

Next, Grant's mother peeked her head in, followed by a lass probably about five years younger than she, just the age her last maid had been when everything had gone wrong. A lump formed in her throat. She pulled the cat closer and pushed the memories away, determined to face this head-on but stay detached at the same time.

Straightening, she smiled and stood, still holding the kitten as a shield. "Hello. I'm Isobel."

The girl walked forward and curtsied slightly. "I'm Annis, and I'm pleased to come work for ye. I went with my cousin to Inverness and had training in how to be a lady's maid."

"I'm sure ye will do just fine."

"Should we get started straight away?" Annis sounded eager.

"I think so, but I havenae even unpacked yet."

"No' a thing to worry over. I'll help." As the girl moved over to the trunks, Grant's mother stepped forward. She'd been having a lovely conversation with the woman the previous evening and was finding her company quite enjoyable until her son had blurted out how he didn't want her in his bed.

Isobel asked, "Do ye have another room I can sleep in? Ye ken yer son doesnae want me here."

"Och, he wants ye here, but I agree, 'twill do him some good to realize what he's done."

She smiled, relief washing over her.

"I have the perfect place for ye to stay until yer ready to come back to this room."

"Thank ye. Why does he think his first wife would have hated me?"

"Because 'twas her brother who died."

Now she was even more confused. "When?"

"On the way to that meeting in Edinburgh."

Her thoughts once again turned to the skirmish on the road. "But I didnae kill anyone that day."

Grant's mother only shrugged.

Let him think her a heartless beast, then maybe he'd let her go. She wasn't going to do anyone any good and there were people here who would try to make her feel again, and what if she couldn't protect them? A shudder ran down her spine.

If she did as her husband wished and didn't attract his attention, he wouldn't bed her and if he didn't, maybe he would lose interest in her and let her go. The best course was to let this maid mold her into a proper wife so she could get out of here as soon as possible.

Chapter Eight

After leaving Isobel with his mother and the new maid, Grant kept himself busy, sitting in on discussions with his father, then heading out to the lists to let some of his frustrations out. Thankfully, his friend Ian was more than happy to oblige.

While in mid-thrust, his friend skidded to the side, smirked, and said, "I saw yer wife out here this morning."

Caught off guard, he faltered for a moment, which was enough for Ian to smack the wooden practice sword on his back. Groaning, he straightened and faced the man head-on. "'Tis no' proper for a lady to be doing such things."

"She seemed to handle herself quite well." Ian chuckled. Grant thrusted and his friend deflected the blow meant to connect with his side in retaliation as he dutifully ignored the man's verbal jab. He continued, "She's nothing like Lyall."

"Nae she is no'." Swinging hard, he aimed the blow to land on Ian's shoulder, but his friend deflected yet again.

"I think that's a good thing."

He stopped. "Lyall was the perfect wife."

"Aye, she may have been, but ye two seemed indifferent

to each other."

"What does that mean?" Grant tightened his grip.

Angry now, he returned to their sparring and sliced through the air to collide with Ian's practice sword, the sound of wood splintering and cracking as Ian explained, "It's like ye were both doing yer duty but there were no emotions involved." Looking down at his damaged sword, Ian shrugged then leveled him with a playful gaze. "I see a spark of interest when ye look at Isobel."

"Are ye sure 'tis no' loathing ye see?" A laugh bubbled in his chest, but it didn't quite make it to the surface.

"If ye truly hated her, ye would have found a way to get rid of her."

He'd had no choice, or at least that's what he'd told himself. But there was something about his wife that had piqued his interest, which had begun on the road to Edinburgh.

"I see it when she looks at ye as well." His friend didn't let up.

"What do ye see?" *Twack*. Ian's wooden blade split in two just as it collided with his leg. *Damn*, the man knew how to throw him off balance.

He couldn't even be angry because he was so stunned at Ian's next words. "That ye two are going to fall hard for each other."

• • •

After returning to the keep, he went to his room and cleaned up. Isobel's trunks had been removed and he smiled, glad she was becoming more established. Maybe his friend was right and they could make this work. Ian was wrong about one thing, however: he might have to share a bed with Isobel, but he would never give her his heart.

That evening, strolling into the hall, he found his wife

sitting next to his mother, but she looked different. The maid had worked. Thank God he didn't have to imagine her clothes falling from her body any longer. But as he got closer, he realized it wasn't going to help.

Isobel's light chestnut locks were pulled up, a tendril escaping and framing her high cheekbones, calling attention to her exposed neck where tiny traces of his mark lingered on display for others to see. When she glanced up at him, he noticed for the first time how long and dark her lashes were, giving her eyes a sultry exotic appeal. She was dressed as a lady should be, but his thoughts turned to mussing up the hair and pulling those full red lips onto his.

The changes didn't stop there. Her gown had been tied properly, but instead of giving her a more sedate, demure appearance, it pushed her breasts up and into focus. He hadn't realized before how large they were. Suddenly, he wanted his hands on them, his mouth on them.

Annis might have to return to the village, because her work had not lessened his desire for his wife, it had increased it. Disgusted with himself, he tore his eyes from her and took the seat near his father, several down from Isobel.

"Have ye thought any more on yer trip?"

"I spoke to Ian today. He, Owen, and Boyd are going to come with us."

"And ye'll take yer wife?"

"Aye." He guessed he'd have to take Annis now, too; obviously it had been a mistake to force a maid upon his wife, but he couldn't think of an excuse to send her away.

"Ye willnae have long before the rest of the signatures reach Edinburgh. If ye wish to convince our Parliament not to accept this agreement with England's, ye will have to make haste."

"We shall leave in two days. I think 'twill give us enough time to prepare. I may be delayed returning."

"Why is that?"

"I need to seek out the man who kens Isobel was with the Resistance."

"Do ye think he will tell Argyll?"

"Since it appears he hasnae yet, I'm hoping he'll be open to a peaceful solution."

His father shook his head. "Ye ken 'tis yer wife's life we're talking about if the man goes to the earl? And if he comes for her the whole clan will defend her."

"I have to try."

"I dinnae want war. If he is not amenable, ye may have to take his life."

"I ken what has to be done and will be prepared if need be."

As he finished dinner, Isobel and his mother stood to leave the table. His gaze was drawn to her waist as she left the room, which was small in comparison to her well-formed hips. His last wife had been tiny and frail—he'd had concerns she might not survive giving him an heir. Isobel's body seemed as if it was made for him to grip her waist and pull her down on top of him, and her hips looked wide enough to comfortably carry many a bairn.

He needed to do his duty and carry on the MacDonald legacy. Tonight was a good night to start. After taking one last swig of ale, he wiped his mouth then set the empty cup back on the table and made his way toward his chamber to claim his wife.

He was surprised to discover Isobel missing. Even the small things that belonged to her on the dressing table were gone. He marched over and opened the wardrobe where her clothes should be hanging. Nothing.

His wife was gone.

• • •

"Where is she?"

When Isobel heard Grant's thunderous voice boom, she flattened her back against the door of the room just across the hall from her husband's.

"She will be returned to yer room when ye provide her with a bed she can be comfortable sleeping in." Fenella MacDonald's soft but stern voice, just audible, crept through the crevices around the wooden frame that had been bolted from within. She was growing quite fond of Grant's mother.

"What?"

"'Twas an awful thing to say that Lyall wouldnae have wanted her in it. Did ye even think how that would make a lass feel?"

There was no reply from Grant.

"She has the right to be given a fair shot at being a good wife to ye, and I willnae let ye make her think she is anything less than yer first wife."

Still no response, and she wished for just a moment she could see his face.

"Have ye even gotten to ken her yet? She's actually quite nice. A bit shy, but I can tell she has a good heart."

The kitten at her feet started to meow. Afraid it would give her away, Isobel picked it up and held the creature close.

Grant's voice was more subdued, but it still carried through the hall. "Ye havenae seen her wield a sword against a man in a battle she had nae place being in."

"Are ye angry that she is a warrior or that she is capable of defending herself without yer help?"

"Nae, ye ken that isnae true."

"Then figure out what bothers ye so because she's no' going anywhere, and until ye admit that and leave the past where it belongs, she can stay in another room."

A light tapping filtered under the door as Grant's mother retreated down the hall. Shortly after, the door on the other side of the hall slammed shut. Closing her eyes, she said a quick prayer of thanks then made her way toward the bed that had once been Grant's cousin's.

Relaxed now, she undressed down to her shift and crawled beneath lush green covers woven from luxurious threads that cradled her flesh in soft relaxing warmth. The cat snuggled in beside her. Sleep evaded her and when it did come, visions of a lass she'd never met taunted her. The woman said she would never have Grant's heart, that she was a monster, and that she looked like a boy. Then came the dreams that Annis was being attacked and there was nothing she could do to defend the lass because a cow sat on her chest and she couldn't breathe.

• • •

The next morning, she awoke to a light rapping on the door just before Annis let herself in with the key Grant's mother had given her.

"Good morning," she said as she sat up and stretched.

"Good day to ye. Did ye sleep well?"

"Aye," she lied. No need to tell the lass she'd had dreams the girl had been attacked and she'd done nothing to help.

"I think the blue dress will do nicely today. What do ye think?"

"Sure 'tis fine." She really didn't care what color she wore.

"Yer kitten is playful this morning."

"Aye, but 'tis nae mine. Can ye help me find it a home? I cannae care for it."

"Why no'? Ye seem to be doing a great job and it loves ye."

She wanted to say *because things I care for always end up hurt*, but she held her tongue as she picked up the cat and pulled it in close.

"Ye should give it a name."

"That would mean I was keeping it. I couldnae do that." She set the kitten down as Annis pulled the gown over her head.

"I think the laird's wife wishes to show ye around some more today."

She nodded. Nimble fingers tightened her laces, and she took a seat at the dressing table.

"Is this place like yer last home?"

"Aye, 'tis very similar."

Och, she wished the girl would stop talking because she was adorable and innocent and charming and would be utterly helpless if a threat was near. After what felt like ages of the girl's chatter, poking, and tying of ribbons, Annis let her up from the chair.

"Ye look lovely."

What was the girl thinking? No one ever said anything like that to her. "I look like a boy."

"And who told ye that? 'Tis nae true. Ye are very bonny."

"Thank ye." She wasn't going to argue with the lass who had apparently made it her mission to pretend that, along with being a good wife, Isobel could actually be desired by someone.

As she studied her hair in the mirror, pinned up at impossible angles with intricately threaded ribbons, she asked, "What happened to Grant's first wife? Nae one has told me, and I dinnae feel right asking him."

"Oh, aye. It makes sense, they wouldnae want to talk about it. She was a wee thing and didnae look healthy from the start." Chills spread through her arms as Annis continued, "They were only married a couple of months. There was nothing to be done for her. She'd been coughing when she arrived and just got worse until she wasted away."

"Did he love her?" Of course he did. Why would she even

ask? The man had insisted his previous wife would dislike her.

"I dinnae ken. I think 'twas an arranged marriage like yers, but he was good friends with her brother, the MacPherson heir. The two were inseparable when they got together. 'Twas always fun to watch the pair of them when the MacPhersons came to visit—Tomas always getting them into trouble, and Grant always finding the way out."

She remembered hearing the MacPherson heir had died in the melee where her husband and she had met for the first time. Maybe he thought the Resistance had started the conflict, and it was his reason for hating her.

Glancing at her face in mirror, she didn't recognize herself. She looked like the lady her mother had always wanted her to be. Had this been her parents' plan all along? She wouldn't put it past them. Smiling, she touched her temple; the curled tresses Annis had left loose bounced gleefully.

For a moment, she was the little girl who had wanted this world, had held hope for the future, and thought it was enough to be a lady and do her duty as a wife. But then Annis came to stand beside her, beaming, holding out the scent she always wore, the one that reminded her of the past and what she had lost, when she had stopped looking in mirrors and dreaming of a peaceful, happy life.

"I found this in yer chest. 'Tis a lovely scent, and I think it matches ye perfectly."

"Thank ye." Her smile faded as she took the bottle and applied the jasmine oil to her wrists and neck.

Gazing at the mirror one more time, she sighed and shook her head. The lass looking back at her let bad things happen to people she loved. It wasn't who she was anymore. Isobel turned her back on the reflection.

Chapter Nine

Sleep had evaded Grant. Why would his mother take his wife away from him? Didn't she understand that would make him want her more? Of course she did—that's what she'd done with anything he'd not appreciated as a child. It worked every time.

Was she trying to teach him a lesson? As he tossed and turned all night, he'd come to the conclusion that it had been in poor taste for him to compare his wives. They were nothing alike, neither were the circumstances for their marriages. Isobel deserved fair treatment and a chance to prove herself.

Taking the steps two at a time down into the hall for breakfast, he thought on the days ahead. He might not be with her tonight, but his mother wouldn't be able to separate them on the journey to Edinburgh. He'd have Isobel mostly to himself. Of course he had to bring a couple men and Annis, but he would manage to get her alone.

As he sat at the table, a serving lad brought in a trencher piled with eggs and breakfast meats. He should probably enjoy them now, because on the trip there would be days where they would need to set up camp and would have only the provisions they took.

As he shoveled in a bite of eggs, his gaze was caught by a flurry of heads turning toward the entrance. His gaze landed on a bonny lass standing in the entryway, and he stopped chewing. It was Isobel.

Without her hair falling all about her face, he was able to enjoy her large sultry eyes, long regal neck, and full pouty lips. She was studying the room as if deciding where to go, like she had a choice. She wasn't shy often, but that bit of uncertainty was alluring.

"Isobel," he called across the room then tilted his head toward the seat at his right. A tentative smile broke across her lips and she started toward him.

Her dress had been laced properly and the fit of her gown hugged her waist, accentuating the curves that lay beneath. His hands itched to wrap fingers around that waist and pull her naked form down onto this. His last wife had looked as if she would break with any sudden movement, while Isobel looked as if she were built for pleasing a man.

"How did ye sleep, husband?"

"Nae well wondering where ye were."

She reddened and turned away just as a lad appeared with a plate for her. "Ye dinnae want me there anyway."

"On the contrary. I have decided I dinnae have to like ye to enjoy the benefits of being married to ye." *Damn*, why had he said that? She did have some redeeming qualities and he'd missed their banter the previous evening. Maybe in time they would grow fond of each other, but telling her he didn't like her wasn't going to improve their relationship.

Isobel's cheeks turned a pretty shade of rose, and he decided he rather liked the look on her face, so he kept up the conversation he was interested in. Expecting the answer would be "no" from her lack of experience kissing, he asked,

"Have ye ever been with a man before?"

As he expected, the flush deepened, and her gaze drifted down to her plate. "I havenae."

Suddenly, he felt guilty again. She was innocent and he was goading her. But he was curious how, after the rumors he'd heard, she was still a maiden. According to the whispers floating around the Highlands, the lass with the Royalist Resistance made camp with the other men.

"And how did ye manage that on all yer nights camped out with the Resistance?"

"I slept with a knife, and most men would stay away, worried they would incur the wrath of..." She trailed off.

Had there been a man who looked out for her, then? Did they care for each other? An irrational anger washed through him. "Who was he?"

"'Tis no' important."

"It is if I have reason to believe some man may come and try to take ye."

"He was like a brother, nothing more."

He didn't press, but decided to ask again when she was more comfortable opening up to him.

"We will be traveling to Edinburgh tomorrow." He'd apparently caught her off guard, and she didn't say anything, so he continued, "Parliament is planning a vote on the Solemn League and Covenants. Have ye heard of them?"

She nodded.

"I hope to be able to convince them 'tis no' in Scotland's best interest to get involved with the English war."

"Do ye think they will listen?"

"I dinnae ken, but I have to try. I will also try to locate this Campbell man while we are on our journey."

"He is probably looking for me."

"I'm hoping I will be able to persuade him to guard your identity. I'm willing to broker some type of truce with him."

"He will never agree." When she shook her head, her curls bounced playfully.

"I want ye to stay out of it and let me handle it."

"I can help."

"Nae, ye cannae." He was aware Isobel could handle herself in battle and had even enjoyed observing her form in the lists yesterday. He'd thought for a moment she looked wild and untamable, like the mountains and pines of his home: strong, formidable, and beautiful. He would probably enjoy sparring with her, but on that fateful day, he'd watched helplessly as the Campbell man had sliced her arm. His stomach lurched at the vision that intruded. He pushed the image away.

"Will ye let me carry a sword to defend myself?" Dressed like she was she had nowhere to hide a weapon, and she needed to appear as if she would never have been near battle. And he couldn't trust her not to run after the man who would turn her over to the Covenanter leader.

"Nae."

"A knife?"

If he reassured her they would be safe, maybe she would voluntarily give up the dangerous life. "'Tis nae need. Ye and Annis will be well guarded."

Panic flashed in her eyes. Did not having a sword really scare her?

"Nae. Annis must stay here," Isobel insisted. "If we are looking for a Campbell, she could get hurt."

"She'll be fine. And she is coming."

"Why?" Isobel's rosy cheeks had paled.

"Because we will see important people, and ye will need to look like a lady, no' the wench who would cut their throats if they dinnae agree with ye."

Pausing with her fork in the air, she tilted her head and a rosy hue returned to her cheeks. "Ye are mistaken if ye think that is who I am."

"Ye are incorrect if ye think I'm fooled by yer new appearance. I ken who ye are. But this is our opportunity to make ye appear so and prove ye cannae be part of that group."

He had a hard time believing her, and he'd had enough of this sparring. It made him want to plant his lips on hers until she couldn't speak, and he wanted that crimson on her face to come from a heated exchange of another kind.

Pushing back his chair, he stood. "Be ready to leave at first light tomorrow."

Taking the stairs back up to his room, he alighted into the hallway on his way to make sure he had everything in hand for the trip. Movement caught his eye and he stopped. Annis came from his cousin Skye's room and walked toward the steps at the front of the castle.

Sliding down the hall, he made his way to the room and peeked in. He pulled open the door and walked over to the dressing table to inspect the contents. A bottle caught his eye, and picking it up, he sniffed it and was rewarded with that exotic scent that was all his wife.

After replacing the stopper, he strolled casually around the room, inspecting it before stopping at the key that hung next to the door. Taking it into his hand, he smiled as he walked through the door, shutting it behind him.

• • •

Isobel followed the cat into the kitchen. She had to find someone who would care for the creature while she was gone and if she was lucky, maybe they would keep it. But her main reason for being here was to find a dirk. She had the small one under the nightstand in Grant's room, but it was better suited for cutting a tender potato than wielding in battle. Grant was crazy if he thought she would leave Annis's and her safety up to people she barely knew.

Letting Annis do her job so far had not worked—his gaze still roamed over her body as if he wanted her as a man desired a woman. Her husband had admitted to not liking her, but he'd apparently decided that wouldn't stop him from taking her to his bed.

Swallowing, she acknowledged if she had to give her maidenhood to anyone, her husband was a well-built, bonny man. And he smelled good, like the air after a rain or the woods of a pine forest. The kiss they had shared was testament to his ability to please a woman. Would he care if she liked their bed play or would he seek to only satisfy his urges and toss her aside?

Thankfully, with his mother's help to move her to another room, she'd been able to delay the inevitable, but once this journey began, he would want to claim his rights or seek out another woman to fulfill his needs. For some reason, that choice angered her.

After spending the day exploring the castle and grounds with Fenella, she'd concluded the Isle of Skye and Cairntay provided the MacDonalds with a fortification she'd only have dreamed possible. The imposing towers of the castle along with the tall cliffs of the landscape that overlooked the churning waters of the channel gave this land advantages over its enemies. It was also beautiful, filled with pines, oaks, and hedges in the most vibrant and varied shades of green. She'd even caught whiffs of wild lavender and occasionally saw the purple-colored bushes dotting the meadows and hillsides.

After enjoying the late meal she strolled into her room and stopped. It somehow looked different. Her items were gone, the mirror was smaller, and the wood dressing table looked darker.

Her gaze landed on the bed and she inhaled sharply—it

was her husband's and his first wife's. The rooms had been switched. *Och*, that meant he'd probably found the knife she'd secured.

Chills spread down her spine as the door behind her clicked then glided open. A rush of cool air enveloped her. She was afraid to turn; a charged current in the room made her scalp prickle. It must be Grant behind her. She swallowed just before arms wrapped around her waist and drew her into a solid frame.

His warm breath filled her ear and his gruff voice said, "Tonight, ye will come back to our room, wife. 'Tis time we made this marriage real."

Chapter Ten

Isobel trembled as her husband released her and backed away. She didn't have a fear of what was to come, so why was she shaking? She'd seen what men and women did in the light of the campfires and had an idea of how it would go. She was a married woman now, and it was time she stopped living as a child.

He reached out and took her hand. The moment felt more intimate than the kiss they had shared; it was an acknowledgment that she trusted him and he, in turn, was asking for that trust. He didn't gloat or make her feel as if she were anything less than him.

In this moment, they weren't two enemies with a shared past, but two strangers making a commitment toward a truce that would guide them through the years ahead. They were like thunder and rain, both fierce forces coming together to form the perfect storm.

"I have to tell Annis no' to…"

"Dinnae worry about her. I told her I would help ye tonight."

His hand was warm and strong, reassuring as he drew her out the door and across the hall to their room.

As the door swung in, she could see not only had the furniture been exchanged, but it was rearranged, with the bed on a separate wall. It had a different feel. It was still light outside, but he'd drawn the curtains and lit candles on either side of the bed.

After guiding her inside, he closed and bolted the door. She moved to the dressing table and touched the tip of her perfume bottle as she inspected the rest of her belongings, which had been laid out across it.

Her gaze drifted up to see Grant, still near the door, his steady stare lingering on her, studying her movements. "I'm sorry about what I said. Lyall was a good woman. She would have liked you."

The mention of his late wife chilled her like jumping into a loch in February. She shut her eyes. When she opened them, he was in front of her, reaching out and taking both of her hands. "I'm telling ye because she wasnae here long. This room is as much yers as it ever was hers. And ye can do with it whatever ye like."

She nodded.

"What I really want to say is we should start over. Let's ken each other."

But she never let herself get close to anyone. He didn't know what he was asking for.

Giving what she hoped was an acquiescing smile, she squeezed his hand. She might be able to share her body with him, but that was it—she had nothing other than that to offer. His words said he was a man of peace and he could be a good husband who would provide and care for her and a family, but the girl who truly believed in those things had been lost a long time ago.

Still, he deserved her acceptance and admiration. She

could give him that.

"Aye." The word finally escaped her lips.

His hands left hers and drifted up her arms, gooseflesh erupting in their wake as he made his way to her temples. "I want to run my fingers through yer hair."

Pins and ribbons fell to the floor as he plucked them out and her tresses unwound in a flurry of curls that fell to her waist. Fingers spread into her hair and massaged against her scalp. She almost moaned at the sensations that rocked through her, nothing like the poking and prodding when Annis had installed them.

His hands cradled the back of her head and tilted it toward his as he dipped his mouth to claim hers. It was no tentative kiss, it was demanding and needy, and the sensation of his lips on hers sent waves of something she couldn't name spreading into her core, heating her and making her wish for more. When his tongue darted in to claim hers, she met it with her own. A hunger awoke in her as she let her hands come up and land on his waist.

He groaned, one hand falling to her back and drawing her in while the other continued to cup her head to keep her close. The melding of their mouths was like magic, a connection she'd never let herself experience with anyone. That sensation elicited a trust she hadn't let herself feel in... well, since the horrid incident which changed her life.

Their tongues continued to dance. He tasted of ale and honey and something so masculine and pure she didn't think this one kiss would be enough. His fingers fisted in her hair and he pulled her deeper as he tilted sideways and ground his body into hers.

Releasing slowly, he drew back. His heated gaze pinned her with an emotion she couldn't name, couldn't explain, except it made her insides quiver. There was a hint of confusion as well, like he'd not expected the intensity at which their connection burned.

His fiery stare drifted to the front of her gown and then he looked offended before he swirled her around, took her hair, and moved it over her shoulder. He worked at the laces down her back as his lips came near her ear. "I've thought of nothing else today but pulling this from your body and seeing my wife for the first time."

His voice was gravelly and raw and twisted her into a tense knot of desire that wanted him to continue whatever course he was on, even if it meant her getting close to someone.

As the gown loosened, instead of feeling like she could breathe, her skin felt tighter, like a tree bending with a fierce wind. Her breasts were heavy and full, engorged and crying out for attention. Grant pulled at the material and drew it over her shoulders, leaving her in her shift and slippers.

Then, he let go of her and she felt cold and abandoned. He pulled off his boots, tossing them to the side before reaching to unbelt his plaid. The space between them gave her clarity and brought back the awareness that had fled with his touch. This man was about to take from her the one thing she'd never allowed anyone. Would it open her up to hurt?

Swallowing, she became riveted on his powerful calves when the tartan material fell from his body. Gaze drifting upward, she followed the curvature of his legs as the exposed muscles gleamed like dark marble in the low, flickering light of the candles. If she touched them, would she feel the strength beneath?

"Isobel."

She met his dark blue gaze but she couldn't speak, could barely breathe as her mouth fell open, wishing for another one of those kisses.

"Yer slippers and stockings." It was a moment before she understood he wanted her to remove them. She nodded, kicking out of the slippers then bending to take one stocking off at a time.

Once she was upright, Grant guided her back and pinned her between his hard body and the wall. He'd removed his shirt. The smoldering heat of his skin radiated through her shift as his chest ground against hers.

Hands grasped onto her thighs then rose, lifting her shift as they made their way up her body. Grant drew away long enough to peel the material over her head. She thought he'd return to kissing her, but his focus lingered on her body and shivers wracked her. The loss of his heat and the cool stones at her back brought with it an awareness of what they were doing, and embarrassment washed over her body.

Would he stop now that he knew what she looked like beneath the frills of a gown?

Sapphire eyes darkened as they studied her breasts. She shielded them with her arms, but his hands clasped around her wrists, steering them to her side, and his head descended to her neck. He suckled and nibbled as he worked his way down to one breast. When his teeth scraped across her nipple, she arched into him.

After lavishing it with attention, he stood and let his body connect with hers, his hard staff pushing against the base of her belly. She gasped and her eyes flew wide as she felt how rigid he was.

Then he moved away, as if the moment was over and he was done with her. She had known she would do something to ruin the moment.

• • •

Grant had almost thrust into his innocent wife up against a cold stone wall—he'd lost awareness of everything except wanting to be inside her. Thank God she'd gasped when she did, or he might have taken her too hard and too fast.

He'd want to do this again and the last thing he should do was scare her.

Although she wasn't the wife he'd chosen, he wasn't heartless.

He closed his eyes and imagined the feel of a cold loch, anything to tamp down this need and keep him from taking things too fast. When he opened his eyes, he saw sadness in her brown gaze and for some reason that bothered him. Why did he care what she thought other than wanting her to desire him all the time?

She started to walk away. He reached out and took her shoulder. "Nae." He drew her in. "This way."

Guiding her toward the bed, he was pleased he'd fought off the urge to pick her up and run for the mattress. The innocence in her eyes said she was fragile right now. The warrior woman who could take down a man with one swipe of her blade had a soft side that she didn't allow anyone to see.

"Lie down," he instructed, and she didn't argue as she backed onto the bed. "A little farther."

She complied, following his lead, not taking her gaze from his body. She looked wary, but more curious. He was glad she no longer tried to cover her body. It glowed in the dancing candlelight, a flashing invitation like a beacon on a cold, dark night.

He liked this side of her, this compliant vixen who opened up to him as she waited for his cock to claim what no other man had. The thought sent a rush of heat through him, and he had to remind himself yet again to slow down. She was untouched.

After climbing onto the bed, he sank down on an elbow next to her as his fingers roamed over her curves. She shuddered and arched into his touch as his hand skimmed across her belly to clasp onto her breast. He had never been with a woman who bowed into his hands, begging for more attention.

Lowering his head, his mouth landed on her mound, kissing at first, then flicking his tongue over her nipple and finally nipping to see what her reaction would be. She moaned and her hands fisted into the covers.

Smiling, he did it again and she reacted the same way. "Do ye like that?"

"Aye. I do." Her breathy response was almost enough to push him over the edge, make him want to plunge in and forge ahead with all his strength, relieving the ache between his legs that had become painful with his desire for Isobel.

His hand explored more, gliding farther down, back across her belly and to the apex of her legs that she had squeezed together, the only sign she was apprehensive about what was to come.

"Open," he said, and he pushed one leg to the side.

He studied her soulful, chocolate eyes as his fingers delved toward her sweet spot; he saw shock and wonder there, until he let one finger caress her slick folds. Her eyes fluttered back as he continued to stroke her woman's area, then he let one finger slide into her. She gasped and her eyes became unfocused, like she was dizzy and falling to pieces on the solid bed beneath her.

It undid him, his cock jerking painfully.

He had to feel her wrapped around him, but he also wanted to watch her come undone. Pulling his hand free, he shifted and climbed up, positioning himself above her. Panic lit her gaze, and she shut her eyes.

"Look at me, Isobel." This was not the killer he'd seen on the battlefield, she was all woman, soft curves, and a trusting heart. He wanted to remember this moment, that she was more than he'd expected.

She obeyed, opening her eyes and meeting his gaze

straight on.

"'Twill only hurt briefly. I'll stop at any time ye wish."

Once she nodded, he positioned his swollen cock at her entrance, running it up and down her passage a couple times to absorb the liquid that had pooled at her core. Her hands came up to rest on his sides as her eyes briefly darted to where they were about to join and then back to his unwavering attention.

As he entered her, her hands tightened, which reminded him to go slow, give her time to adjust and expand to meet his demands. When he came up against the barrier that reaffirmed her innocence, he waited only a second before plunging through, all the way in one burst, then resting, deep inside her, letting her recover. She only flinched, but her curiosity dimmed.

He wanted it to return. "Are ye all right?"

"Aye," she said, but she didn't move, so his head dipped to her mouth, claiming it, and doing his best to make her forget the pain, to bring back the pleasure and desire that had driven him onward.

When she started matching the strokes of his tongue, he knew he had accomplished his goal. Then his mouth wandered to her sensitive throat, the place that had taunted him with his mark the last couple of days. Now, she was fully his. He didn't need to mark her to know it.

He sucked and nibbled until she was once again arching into him. Slowly, he rotated his pelvis gently, afraid if he pulled out, he would plunge back in and frighten her. Isobel's hips writhed beneath him, matching his assault as if on instinct. It drove him mad.

She whimpered, a low mewing noise that indicated she was receiving as much pleasure as he. As he rocked, she gasped and threw her head back. He did it again and she fell to pieces beneath him. It was the most beautiful sight he'd ever seen, her bonny eyes fixated on him as what he did to her pulled her under.

He felt the pressure build as one wave of sensation rocketed through him, then another and still more as his whole body was wracked with burst after burst of ecstasy so intense he lost the world around him. As his seed filled her, he may have called out her name, but he wasn't sure.

The room came back into focus. He held himself up then withdrew and rolled next to her, because he didn't want to flatten her beneath his weight.

Lying beside her, he came to the conclusion he'd made the right choice by indulging in her favors. She was his, after all. He would have to change her; she didn't have to be the barbarian from the melee. There was a softer side to her, he just had to figure out how to make her this new woman and leave the old one behind. He might even one day forgive her if she gave up her savage ways.

Chapter Eleven

Isobel was afraid to move as the sun rose the next morning. Her husband still lay beside her, their bare skin touching, one arm slung over her belly. She had to relieve herself, but didn't want him to see her in full daylight, so staying beneath the covers seemed like a good idea.

She couldn't handle the shame if he looked upon her and decided he no longer wanted her. And now that she knew how pleasant bed play could be for a woman, she was afraid he might turn her away. She ached between her legs, but what she'd experienced last night had made it worth every second.

Grant's fingers started dancing on her skin, making gooseflesh arise and take hold of her body. When she glanced over, his gaze was on hers.

He smiled and asked, "How did ye sleep?"

"Well. Ye?"

He groaned and rolled onto his side as if he planned to climb on top of her, but all he did was study her. A warm flush gripped her. *Och*, what must her tangled mess of hair look like?

"Ye should eat well this morning. I'm nae sure where we'll be stopping along the way, and the provisions we bring with us will be more to fill our bellies than for taste."

She was used to that, hiding in the woods with the Resistance, but she didn't want to remind him of her involvement with the group. Not now, when he seemed to be pleased with her.

"I'll send Annis in to see ye are ready."

"Does she ken we are leaving? Did she have time to pack for herself?" Isobel's mind started racing with ways to keep the lass comfortable.

"Aye. I told her."

Drawing back the covers, he started to scoot from the bed, but stopped short, staring down at his manhood then to the bed where they had been snuggled together. Her cheeks reddened when a small staining of blood caught her eyes. Looking away, pretending to still be sleepy, she was relieved he said nothing and rose to dress.

When his boots hit the floor and stopped at the door, she studied him where he was, hand on the knob, staring at the exit. He looked as if he wanted to say something. Instead, he opened the door, walked out, and shut it quietly behind him.

It felt like mere moments before a light knock sounded.

"'Tis Annis," the maid called out.

"Enter." She sat up and as Annis pushed in the door, a little blur ran in and jumped onto the bed, nearly missing the top, but digging in its claws and climbing the rest of the way. "Good morning," she said to her maid as she rubbed the creature's neck.

"My sister is going to collect yer kitten to watch while we are gone. She'll return her when we get back."

"She isnae my kitten. Does yer sister want to keep her?" The creature was already rubbing its head against hers and making that adorable sound.

"Nae, they have too many animals already."

"How do ye ken it's a girl?"

"I looked. Ye should give her a name."

No, she couldn't do that. She didn't want a cat. How was she to get rid of the thing? She stroked its head and the wee creature pushed up into her hand. She'd have slept with it last night, except she'd been with her husband. A blush stole across her face.

"I was told to pack light. We willnae be taking a carriage."

Good, because she'd felt claustrophobic the few times she'd been in one. She much preferred the open air where she could see threats if one came upon them.

Realizing she was still naked beneath the covers, she scanned the room for her shift. It was near the far wall where Grant had peeled it from her body last night, along with her gown, slippers, and stockings. *Och*, what a mess, and now Annis would know.

But she was a married woman. Supposedly, she'd been with her husband on the night of their marriage—it should come as no surprise to the lass. Pulling the blankets close, she swallowed. "Will ye please bring my shift?" She pointed to the wadded-up material.

"Aye. I'm sorry I wasnae here to help ye last night."

"Nae, 'twas no problem."

A knock sounded. Annis said, "Ah, 'twill be Fergus. Yer husband sent him to retrieve water for ye to bathe before our journey."

It surprised her Grant took the time to see to her needs. She smiled, anticipating the warm water.

Half an hour later, Isobel was clean and Annis had dressed her in a dark green gown with her hair pulled up. She headed down to break her fast.

As she strolled into the great hall, she saw her husband seated next to the laird. With a deep breath, she made her way toward them and eased into the chair next to Grant.

"But ye ken that wouldnae have stopped him," the laird said, his expression sad. As Grant shook his head, his father continued, "There was nothing any of us could have done."

A servant set a plate down in front of her; her husband kept his attention on his father. She nearly flinched when his hand rested on her thigh, a reassuring touch, as if her presence was welcome. A flutter started in her stomach, and she wondered if he could grow to care for her, but she pushed the thrill aside. Thankfully, Grant's mother came in and took the seat next to hers.

"I have a gift for ye." Fenella beamed.

"I have everything I need." She was trying to be polite. No one ever gave her gifts—she wouldn't know what to say if someone gave her something.

Grant's mother took her hand and turned it palm up. She placed a pendant attached to a long gold chain in the center and smiled at her. "I want ye to ken ye belong here, and ye will be loved as if ye were family born to us."

Her eyes began to sting, and Isobel fought an emotion she shouldn't let in. She didn't deserve the kind words or a gift. Glancing down, she studied the pendant. It was an enameled replica of the MacDonald crest, circled by alternating rubies and pearls. Her eyes blurred as she fingered the detailing on it. It was fashioned with a pin so it could be worn as a brooch.

"I cannae accept it." As much as she wanted to belong, she was certain fate was just playing a cruel game on her.

"'Tis yours when ye are ready to wear it. I'm sure this is a tough transition, but when ye are ready, I am here for ye." Grant's mother closed Isobel's fingers around the necklace, leaving the solid weight of it resting in her hand, then she let go and turned to work on the food that had just been set in front of her.

Isobel sat stunned as she held the object under the table,

not sure what to do with it.

The rest of the meal, Fenella spoke about the journey her husband and she were about to make. It was pleasant conversation, and it lulled her into a peace she wasn't sure she wanted, because she couldn't afford to become complacent. The pendant became heavier and heavier in her hand.

. . .

As soon as his wife entered the great hall, Grant looked away. All he could think of was their evening together, and how she'd fallen apart beneath him. Isobel closed the distance and sat next to him. She wore a dark green gown that made her skin glow as if she stood in golden beams from the sun. He rested his hand on her leg, not to pin her as he had on their wedding night, but because there was something reassuring about how easily she'd slid into the space next to him. His cock became hard and painful when he caught a whiff of her perfume.

He didn't look at her because he was finding it difficult to calm the raging desire ignited last night. His father continued his lecture about the uncle he'd lost years earlier. The topic sobered him, and he became more focused.

Leaning in, his father whispered, "Do ye think ye are resisting this match because of what she's done in the past, or because she reminds ye of my brother?"

"They are nothing alike." The denial was out of his lips in an instant, but there was a truth to the laird's statement Grant didn't want to acknowledge.

"Then ye have not stopped to consider why Isobel was fighting for the Resistance. Have ye bothered to ask her?"

"Aye, but she didnae give me a straight answer."

"I bet there is something there ye dinnae see. Take the time to ken who she is while ye are gone. I think she will surprise ye."

Taking his last bite of eggs, Grant thought about his father's words then took a sip of his drink and pushed away from the table. Addressing Isobel, who was engulfed in a conversation with his mother, he interrupted, "We should be ready to go within the hour. I'll meet ye and Annis at our chamber to see what I need to carry down."

Before she had a chance to acknowledge him, he made his way toward the stables to ensure the horses and the men accompanying them were ready. If he'd seen those full red lips, he might have wanted to drag her up to the room and have his way with her one more time before they left. But he'd witnessed the blood this morning. If he took her too soon, it might hurt her. Better to be safe.

As he walked, he enumerated how his wife and his uncle were different.

As a lass, she had no business going into battle, but his uncle had been young and had had no business facing down the MacLeod men who ultimately killed him. If she gave peace a try, she might find it worked, and if his uncle had given peace a try, he might still be alive. Just like his uncle, she had a sharp tongue and strong intellect.

Damn, they were similar.

But unlike his uncle, if she disappeared from his life tomorrow, he wouldn't miss her.

Och, but was that true anymore? He'd not stopped thinking about her since waking, and he'd begun to enjoy their verbal sparring, just as he had enjoyed practicing in the lists with his uncle as a child.

Her reaction to him was what drew him in the most. She'd arched into every caress and movement he'd made, urging him on and calling to a primal part of him he hadn't known existed. He'd never been with a woman who seemed to enjoy bedding as much as she did, and that knowledge sent him to new heights.

His wife was dangerous, but he wanted more.

Owen, Ian's twin brother, was preparing the horses when he walked into the stables. "We will be ready to go within the half hour."

"Great." He asked Ian, who came from one of the stalls, "Do ye think the Royalists have a chance of stopping the Solemn League and Covenant?"

"If there is hope for peace, the other clans will be glad to have ye there by their side." Ian rubbed his hands on his plaid.

"I will need both of yer help."

"With what? I dinnae have the same way with words ye do." His friend laughed.

"With my wife."

Owen turned his head to the side then quipped, "She is quite bonny. I'd be happy to help if ye cannae handle her." A hearty laugh filled the stable.

"'Tis no' what I am asking of ye." Anger lanced him. Giving Owen his best battle-hardened glare made the man back off.

"Ye ken I was jesting?" Owen threw his hands up in the air.

Yesterday, he didn't think the remark would have bothered him. He knew the man was joking, but the thought of another's hands on Isobel's curves made his skin boil.

"What do ye need?" Ian chimed in.

"I am telling ye, because I ken ye two will keep her safe. She was in the Royalist Resistance." Owen whistled just as Boyd strolled up to join the group.

"Nae! I thought she looked familiar." Ian was genuinely surprised.

"I cannae let her meet with them. Someone has guessed her identity, and if they report back to Argyll, he will come for her and the MacDonalds."

His friend shook his head.

"I need help keeping an eye on her, especially while I'm in with Parliament. I dinnae trust her not to get herself into some kind of trouble."

Ian nodded. "Aye. We'll keep an eye on her."

Boyd and Owen agreed.

"And dinnae let her ken ye ken the truth." His gaze strayed over all three men until they nodded.

"I'll go get the ladies. Meet back here in half an hour."

A few minutes later, he was climbing the stairs and striding toward his room. When he opened the door, he found Isobel lying on her side on the bed, stroking the wee kitten. Suddenly, he wanted to be that creature and feel her hands caressing his body.

Annis was absent, so he strode over and sat near Isobel; the motion turned her to face him and she smiled.

Och, it was an invitation if he ever saw one.

Dipping his head to hers, he caught a whiff of her exotic scent just before their lips met. She seemed as eager as he was when he drove his tongue into her mouth. His cock tightened and grew as the embrace became more heated and she arched into him, moaning with a need that matched his own. *Damn*, she knew how to send him off balance.

He was just reaching for the ribbons at the front of her dress when he heard the door swing in. He pulled back and glanced over his shoulder to see Annis stroll into the room.

"I'm sorry. I'll come back later if ye want."

"Nae, 'tis fine. We need to be on our way." He was thankful his plaid covered what his wife had been able to do to him only by being on their bed. Pointing to the satchels by the door, he said, "Is this everything?"

"Aye. There wasnae a lot of room, so we will have to wash frequently."

"I dinnae need all that fancy stuff." Isobel waved her hand dismissively at the satchels.

"Aye, ye will while we are in Edinburgh." He didn't want to add in front of Annis that Isobel needed to look like a soft, stylish lady who would never sully her hands by touching a sword. For the first time, he worried there might be danger in bringing her along. What if Torsten Campbell was looking for her or had told others? If she was recognized, there could be trouble. But if the man had told anyone, Argyll would have already been upon their shores demanding his clan relinquish her.

Turning his attention to something harmless, he asked, "What are ye doing with the cat?"

"I'll drop her in the kitchens until Annis's sister gets here. I'm hoping the girl will decide to keep it."

As he slung the bags over his shoulder, his gaze was caught by Isobel bringing the cat to her cheek and giving it a hug. He didn't know why she wouldn't admit she wanted the thing. He had no problem with her keeping a pet—it might even keep her from wanting to return to the battlefield.

"Let's be on our way," he said.

Standing, Isobel kept the kitten cradled close and made her way through the door, followed by Annis and then him as he pulled the door shut with his free hand.

They stopped in the kitchens to leave the animal, and his wife set it down and ran out as if the wee thing might follow her and cry for more attention. He stifled a laugh. Annis trailed behind, and it occurred to him Isobel might be trying to keep distance between her maid and herself as well. Did the lass just not like people?

After securing the bags to the horses, he helped Annis on her mare then moved toward his wife to find she'd already mounted on her own. She looked so proud sitting there, back straight, head held high. She breathed in and smiled, closing her eyes and soaking in the glowing warmth of the morning sun.

Her hair was pulled up and she looked like a lady, but he wouldn't be fooled by the new appearance. Underneath, she was still the hellion who was rightfully feared by the Covenanters roaming the Highlands. He'd even found a knife she'd hidden in their room. It proved he couldn't yet trust her.

They were only riding the animals down to the ship on the beach. He didn't want to take his new bride along and he wasn't sure if it was because he didn't trust that she wouldn't run off and start a war or if it was because he wanted to drag her back up to their bed and keep her on her back beneath him.

Isobel and Annis followed as he led the way to the horse path and down to the beach, where a ship would carry them across the fast-flowing water that separated the Isle of Skye from the mainland of Scotland. The path was treacherous and steep, but there was not an ounce of fear on Isobel's face while Annis kept her mount as far from the drop as possible.

How different his first wife was from his second. Isobel faced the descent head-on, while Lyall had clung to him and nearly scared the horse they'd been riding into plunging down the side. His wife was well suited to this land. She was wild and untamed, like the jagged rocks of the shoreline and the imposing cliffs and mountains of Skye, a beauty that stole your breath when gazed upon.

Lightning struck in the distance as dark clouds came from the south, the direction they were headed. Cursing the weather, he picked up the pace, the rest of the party following suit, and in no time they were dismounting and boarding the boat for mainland Scotland.

The rain didn't come on softly, it appeared in an instant and pelted down on them like thousands of tiny dirks. Although everyone else ran for cover, his wife stood at the rails, head tilted up to the wet deluge. Some of her hair had fallen free and blew in the wind, making her appear wild and free and untamable. Then she was looking down at the waves, enjoying the dance of the turbulent sea. When her attention shifted to him, she smiled.

An image of his uncle fighting The MacLeod in the pouring rain washed over him. He shuddered, recalling his uncle's head severed then falling to the ground.

Too late, he realized his father had been correct—Isobel was too much like the mentor and friend he'd lost all those years ago.

It had been a huge mistake to bring her on this trip.

Chapter Twelve

By midday, Isobel was tired of the pounding rain, and poor Annis had barely spoken a word. The lass probably didn't have much experience being out in the elements. She could handle it, but a coldness had crept in as soon as she'd seen Grant staring at her like she were a ghost or like he could see through her.

It had been unnerving, and since then he'd put distance between them, not even wishing to help her when they'd mounted their horses again. The man she'd only met this morning, Owen, whose twin, Ian, also rode with them, helped Annis onto her horse.

Sometime in the afternoon, the rain gave them a short break and they huddled around a small area that had been used as a campsite by previous travelers. She sat on a log, stuffing bread and cheese into her mouth, and wished it had been dry enough to start a fire. She shivered and when she glanced up, it was to find Grant watching her. She gave him a weak smile. She was certain she looked like a drowned rat, and her husband would never want her affections again if he was put off by her appearance.

Och, she didn't know why she cared.

Once they finished up, she walked back to her horse. Really, she shouldn't think of the animal that way. It was the same horse she'd ridden into the village the other day, but it belonged to Grant's cousin, not her. And it was better that way, even if the horse neighed and looked at her with big eyes that reminded her of the chocolate she drank as a child on special occasions back home.

She turned away from the beguiling eyes to find her husband beside her, ready to lift her. She smiled and let him, pulling her skirts up so as to ride easier.

Grant stiffened, then his hands were on the bottom of her gown, inching it up to see the knife she had fastened to her thigh. "What the hell do ye think ye are doing?"

"Protection." She leaned down and hissed at him. She didn't want the attention from the others his outburst had generated. The rest of their party was now watching them, although they studiously pretended not to.

"Ye willnae be needing this. Ye have us to protect ye." His fingers deftly untied the cord she'd used to secure the dirk she'd found on her search in the kitchen.

At first she felt anger, but the rain started again, pelting her, and a bone-deep resignation and sadness washed over her. How was she to guard Annis if she didn't have a weapon? She couldn't count on the men to be there.

No one had been there when she needed help.

Her eyes blurred but instead of letting a tear escape and show her weakness, she turned her head as the weight of the weapon slid away. It was replaced by a warm weight on her shoulders as Grant covered her with a dry plaid.

The rain continued the rest of the afternoon, although the pace was slower. It had done its damage to their progress and by the time they found an inn for the night, Annis was ready to fall over with fatigue.

They ate a quick meal in the common area then went above stairs. Grant had secured three rooms, one for Ian, Owen, and Boyd, another for Annis, and the last for himself and her. As soon as the door was shut and bolted, he pulled the laces from her gown and peeled it from her body. He laid it across a chair to dry then removed her shift. She would shiver under his intense gaze, but she actually felt warmer with the wet garments off.

After kicking off her shoes and removing her stockings, she hung them and found Grant was naked, too. He backed her to the bed and they were joined and panting before she knew it.

The next morning, sun shone through the window like the storm from yesterday was a distant memory. When she scooted toward the edge of the bed to rise and retrieve her clothing, Grant drew her back to his hard body and wordlessly took her again. A closeness in his gaze she hadn't seen before pulled her under, intensifying the feelings and odd emotions swirling in her chest as she fell to pieces beneath him.

When he collapsed to the side of her, he traced his fingers along her curves. She blushed then reached to draw the blankets up and hide from his study of her body.

"What are ye doing?" Grant took her hand in his. She let go of the covers and he reached to lay her arm over her head, which pushed her breast up for his viewing.

She tried to pull it back down, but he held it there, gentle but determined. She called on her reserves, the strength that allowed her to not care what others thought, but, exposed to him as she was, it didn't work well, She hated she could feel the warmth creeping up her neck and her face redden. "I look like a boy."

"Why would ye think that?"

"I've always looked like a boy."

Grant's brows knit together. "Ye look nothing like a lad. Is that why ye dress up in men's clothes and fight?"

She tried to turn her face, because the question was not far from the mark and reminded her of that day. The one she wanted to forget. The day she hadn't fought hard enough and had let her world crash around her.

"Nae. 'Tis just what I've been told."

"Well, whoever told ye that is blind. Ye are quite bonny. Even dressed as a boy, 'tis no way ye can hide yer lovely face."

She froze. What was he talking about?

"And these." He trailed kisses across her breasts. His head rose and he gazed at her with blue eyes that made her want to fall into them. "Ye are bonny and dinnae let anyone tell ye different." He planted a quick kiss on her lips then rose and started to dress.

As she pulled on her still damp clothes, she couldn't help but think maybe he didn't hate her. Her heart did this weird flutter, because things never worked out for her—people who cared for her got hurt and left.

The next week continued on in the same way, with them barely having time to speak during the day then coming together at night. But now, she avoided talking, deciding she needed to examine her feelings, because she was developing a fondness for her husband. It might be time to put some distance between them before he had the chance to make her care.

It had been easier to argue with him than to have conversations.

He didn't seem to mind, because he made her body feel like she was a woman each evening and the next day left her to Annis's company while he conversed with his men. But he always kept a watchful eye on her and the maid, and his smile seemed to be given more freely now.

As they traveled, her maid regaled her with tales of

growing up on the Isle of Skye and of the MacDonald clan, even some involving her husband as a mischievous, carefree boy. What had happened to him? He always seemed so serious she couldn't imagine he'd ever done anything without a purpose.

As they neared Edinburgh, she spied a familiar tree laid across the side of the road rotting, and she stopped to examine it. The scar on her shoulder where she'd been sliced by Torsten Campbell's blade burned, and she remembered this was the spot of that skirmish. She tried to recall what had happened to Tomas MacPherson, but the memories remained elusive. She was certain she'd never seen the man.

It was evident Grant knew where they were as well. He stared down at a wooden cross that had been planted on the opposite side of the road. When he looked at her, the sadness in his gaze turned to resentment. Even from several yards away, she could see him shaking and feel rage and despair radiating from him.

Grant turned and trotted off without a word or a backward glance. He was back to his brooding, and he appeared to put distance between them again. Good, because that felt more normal than the flutter in her chest that ached because he blamed her for his loss.

When they stopped for the evening, it was to find the inn only had two rooms available. She would stay with Annis and Grant with the other men, which was fine by her. As she stretched out in one of the two small beds in the room, she fought the emptiness that tried to envelop her. She was becoming accustomed to sleeping near her husband, and that wouldn't do.

Grant brooded the next morning over a quiet breakfast, and she didn't mind. His disgust with her meant there was a chance he'd let her leave, which was exactly what she intended to do. She was not wife or mother material, and she had no desire to examine why the thought of him hating her made her chest feel heavy.

· · ·

Grant hadn't slept. He had almost thrown his arm over Boyd during the night, thinking the man was Isobel. He'd spent the rest of the evening stewing over how comfortable it had become to have her next to him and how he missed it after only one night apart. It was only because his body had become accustomed to spilling his seed inside her each night, he was certain of it.

He'd kept his distance during the day, but as they approached the city, he found himself falling back next to Isobel's side. He would need to keep a close eye on the faces of strangers in Edinburgh to make sure no one recognized her and an even keener one on her to ensure she didn't jeopardize her safety or that of their group.

"'Tis bonny." His wife appraised Edinburgh Castle sitting high atop a hill with cliffs dropping from three sides. One roadway led to the proud, foreboding gate, barring any enemy who dared consider breaching its formidable walls.

"Aye, that it is. Have ye been here before?"

"Nae." Isobel's gaze darted around the city. "We had planned to come for the meeting, but once I was injured on the way here, Alex sent me home."

He hadn't made it to Edinburgh, either—he'd been helping to deliver his friend's body back to MacPherson land. But he'd been here other times and knew the area well.

His hands tightened around the reins, but instead of his thoughts turning to his friend's death, it was the unfamiliar name on his wife's lips that sparked a burning in his chest. It felt similar to the anger he'd felt when his father had praised his cousin for besting him in a sparring match.

"Who's Alex?"

She said nothing.

"Is this the man with the Resistance who looked after ye?"

"Aye."

"Does he have feelings for ye, then?" The sun beat on him, and he could feel his brow heating. She'd told him no before, but she'd held back from him. He needed to be certain.

"Nae. Nothing beyond a familial concern."

How could a man look on Isobel and not want her? "Ye are to stay away from him." The order came out clipped, and he chided himself for not clarifying she was safer staying away from the man. And Alex would really be the one in harm's way if Grant caught him anywhere near his wife.

"Ye willnae tell me who I can speak to," she snapped.

"Ye have already caused enough trouble. If I catch ye with anyone from that group, ye will find yerself locked away at Cairntay."

Isobel's eyes flashed with defiance. "I willnae be caged like an animal."

"I cannae let ye bring war to our clan."

But that wasn't really what worried him, because the MacDonalds were a fierce lot and if Argyll came to their shores, they would be able to defend themselves, especially with their allies, the Cameron clan, to the south. It was more the twist in his gut at the thought of waking without her.

It must be the fear of losing another wife. He had to prove he could keep this one safe. That was it. It had nothing to do with Isobel herself.

Isobel looked over to her maid and stilled, except for a slight nod of the head. Slowly, she turned her gaze back to him. "I willnae put anyone in danger."

He nodded then pulled up to the front of the group, satisfied that his wife would behave. But even if she didn't, he'd worked out a schedule with the men to keep an eye on her. Her innocent eyes didn't fool him for an instant.

Turning his attention back to their surroundings, Grant admired the strength surrounding the castle on the hill. But as they trotted down the busy streets with the sun setting in the distance, he studied the faces of those they passed to see if anyone recognized his wife. None did.

He led the group to find an inn near Greyfriars Kirk, the place where he would present his case to the Scottish Parliament. As the crowds dispersed, he came to an inn called the Drowsy Duckling, where they secured three rooms. He left his wife in one and Annis in another, instructing the lasses to bolt the doors behind him. He met the MacDonald men in the common area.

"Ye will all have a watch on the lasses when I leave for the Kirk in the morning. I'm no' sure when they'll be listening to me and the other clansmen, so we may be here a few days."

"We'll no' let them out of our sights." Boyd raised a glass then pulled it to his lips.

"What are we supposed to do with them? I dinnae think yer wife is going to be pleased with being kept in her room."

"Take them shopping." A collective groan emerged from the group. She'd probably hate it as much as the men, but a fashionable lady was the best cover Isobel could hope to have. "But ye'll have to make sure no one recognizes Isobel. And if they do, ye get her and Annis to safety straight away."

"Where should we take them?"

"If something happens and we get separated, we'll meet back up at the inn at that village we passed just before getting to Edinburgh. Another thing, watch Isobel closely and make sure she doesnae find a weapon. I dinnae want her causing trouble."

After excusing himself, he made his way to the other side of the room to secure some writing instruments from the innkeeper then closed himself in the man's study. He penned a letter to Torsten Campbell, hoping to be able to make his point without anyone else understanding the missive.

Mr. Campbell,

I am pleased to inform ye that I have recently wed Isobel MacLean. Please come to the ferry house near the Isle of Skye and send word when ye have arrived to congratulate our union. I look forward to traveling across the water to neutral land.

I'm sure we also have a mutual interest to discuss how we can both benefit from a peaceful solution to our shared concern.

Grant MacDonald

The letter folded and sealed, he tucked it away and went above stairs to dine with his wife. As he rounded the corner into the hall, he found Isobel pacing the corridor.

"What are ye doing out here?" He scanned the space and relaxed when he saw they were alone.

"I dinnae like her being in there without a guard."

"Who?"

"Annis. Who else?" Her gaze darted back to the door.

"Did she lock the door behind her?"

"Aye, but I still dinnae think 'tis safe in such a place."

"She will be fine. If ye like, I'll have the men take turns keeping watch on all the doors." He'd been rolling the idea over in his mind anyway.

Isobel sighed, but didn't budge. "Well, do ye want to go get someone or should I?"

"I'll be right back." He returned shortly with Ian in tow.

"I can take a shift, too." Isobel wrung her hands.

"Ye will do nae such thing."

"But I can keep everyone safe."

"I'm certain ye can, but if ye've been spotted and a group comes for ye, I'll no' have ye waiting outside alone for them to cart ye off." He turned as footfalls sounded on the steps.

After grabbing hold of her arm, he steered Isobel to their room and opened the door, just as a lass crested the steps with a tray filled with roasted meats and vegetables along with bread and cheese. Stomach growling, he held the door open for the tavern maid to follow Isobel into the room.

Isobel glanced at the tray then looked at him.

"I've had some sent to Annis, too."

She smiled at him, the first one he'd seen in a couple of days.

Once the serving lass had left, he closed the door and bolted it, turning just in time to see his wife attempt to swipe a dirk from the tray. "Put it back."

"Surely ye willnae leave me defenseless while ye are at the Kirk?"

"Nae. Ye will have my men with ye. No need to draw attention to yerself. Ye have to look like a meek lady who would never consider touching such a weapon."

"I dinnae like being dependent on men for my safety or anyone else's."

"'Tis just for a couple days, then we'll be headed back to Skye."

Placing the dirk back on the table, she sat and picked up a plate. He took the seat next to her and slid the knives from her reach.

After eating then retiring for the night, Isobel opened to him and when he entered her, she clung to him and matched every move he made. It was amazing how she'd come to trust him and give of herself so freely.

Lying sated next to her, a strange bliss assailed his senses and he fell asleep with hope that if he could tame his savage wife and he could help make peace in the Highlands.

Chapter Thirteen

Isobel's eyes opened, the bed beneath her shifting with Grant's weight as he rose from the thick mattress. She'd never expected to enjoy the sight of an unclothed man, but she had to admit her husband's form was pleasing. His lean muscled legs led to a tightly sculpted backside that, on many occasions, she'd dug her fingers into to draw him nearer.

He pulled a white shirt over the broad expanse of his shoulders, the sinew and curves that only hours ago had held her and made her feel safe in the dark, the ones her fingertips had memorized.

No. She turned away. What nonsense. He would be gone today, and she would be the one fending off any threats that came her way. She would pretend to be the picture of a perfect lady. But she would not rely on him or any of the other men in their group. Depending on men got people hurt.

Closing her eyes, she pretended to be asleep as she fought the confusion that had come at her so unexpectedly. A moment later, the bed shifted as Grant sat next to her. She kept her eyes sealed while he pushed a stray curl from her face and his fingers trailed down to her neck, delving into the hair at the base of her skull. She already felt heated as he leaned in and placed his lips on hers then withdrew without letting go of her.

Her heart fluttered. What the hell was that? She was not going to let him make her feel, so she opened her eyes to give him a set down. When her gaze met his, she could see he had been seeking comfort, his gaze clouded, probably from worry over his meeting today. So, instead of pushing him away, she said, "Good morn."

Smiling, he placed his lips on hers again, his tongue penetrating as she opened to him. The world washed away as it did each time he drew her into his embrace and made her feel things she'd not known possible. Too soon, he was withdrawing.

"Parliament will be meeting soon. I need to go." Releasing her, he stood.

Suddenly, she felt she needed to be with him, to keep him safe. "Will someone be going with ye?" *Och*, why did she even care?

"Nae. They are going to stay here and take ye to the market for shopping if ye wish."

Her lip curled.

"Or ye can stay here in the room, but either way ye need them with ye for safety. And…ye must act like a perfect lady."

She liked the idea of being caged up in the room even less, so shopping it would be. Maybe while she was out, she could get a lead on where to find Torsten before he found her.

"Ye will need to break yer fast." She rose to sitting and stretched.

"Aye. I'm going to get something quick to take on the walk. The innkeeper is preparing something for the rest of ye that should be ready soon."

She nodded. "What time will ye be back?"

"I dinnae ken." He sauntered toward the door in the crisp shirt and plaid he'd kept hidden in his bag and away from the dust. He looked every bit the Highland warrior and clan chief heir he was. A sense of pride washed over her.

"I wish ye luck." And she truly meant it.

She might not believe the minds of the Covenanters could be changed, but Grant was a strong leader. She'd seen how the MacDonald men looked up to him and were willing to follow him into battle if need be. He had set his sights on trying and his cause was a noble one.

Stopping shy of the exit, he glanced back to her. "Thank ye." His gaze met hers and she knew it had been the right thing to say. "I will be back as soon as I can." He turned and walked out the door, closing it behind him with a soft *thud*.

After sliding from beneath the covers, she donned her shift just before a light rapping at the door announced Annis's arrival. Before long, the maid had her trussed up in a rose-colored bodice with sleeves trimmed with matching bows. The complementing skirt was embroidered with white flowers and weighed more than a heavy claymore strapped to her back.

Why did women wear such things?

She studied Annis's work in the mirror. The lass staring back had rosy cheeks and doe-like brown eyes. Her hair was pinned up, curls and ribbons falling around her face. The tresses bobbed with her movements. She was mesmerized.

"Ye look lovely."

She turned toward Annis. "This isnae me."

"Och, yes it is. Have ye never noticed how bonny ye are?"

"Nae." Her hands trembled as she touched the mirror. She was about to say it was a magic spell when a knock sounded at the door.

Ian called out, "Are ye done in there yet? The innkeeper has our food ready and 'tis getting cold."

Isobel followed her maid to join the men and break their fast.

They spent the rest of the morning strolling in and out of shops, looking at items that bored her, but at the same time had her feeling inadequate. All these things women were expected to wear. Did the finery really make a man lust after a woman the way her husband did? If so, she would wear them anytime, because she quite liked bedding her husband.

Still, this business of being a lady was tedious. But, for her husband, she would pretend to all of Scotland she was incapable of protecting herself and others.

After a while, they ate a light afternoon meal and then strolled down the streets some more. The three MacDonald men flanked Annis and her like they were some sort of prize, but she knew the truth of it. Grant had told them who she was, and they were probably making sure she didn't get in any trouble.

Well, his men ran out of luck, because walking straight toward them was Alex Gordon, the leader of the Royalist Resistance. Of course, these men wouldn't know that because he kept his identity well hidden. She'd accidentally slipped and told her husband, but she'd never tell anyone again.

As he strolled by, she studied him from the corner of her eye. His brow furrowed then recognition dawned, and he tilted his head to indicate a tavern down the street. Now, she just had to shake her guards long enough to see what news he had for her.

"I believe I am in need of some new stockings," she turned to her guards and said. It was probably the truth, but she didn't really know. She hadn't bothered to see what was in her trunks back at Cairntay, but surely the ones she'd brought on this trip were ruined. As she ducked into a crowded shop, her companions were forced to swerve and follow her.

Picking up a pair she gushed, "Och, these are lovely."

Approaching the merchant, she held them up. "Do ye have a place I can try them on?"

"Aye, me lady, straight through here."

"Do ye want me to come with ye?" Annis asked.

"Nae. 'Tis just stockings. I think I can manage."

Looking to the men and Annis, she smiled. "I'll only be a moment. Why dinnae ye wait here?" She pointed to a sitting area in the shop.

Once through the door to the back of the establishment, she handed the stockings back to the lady. "I'm so sorry, but I need to get away for a moment. Do ye have a back door?"

"Aye, miss, but what do I do..."

"Stall them. I'll be back shortly. Can you bring a few pairs in and out and pretend I'm trying them on? I promise to purchase several pairs." That obviously got the woman's attention. She nodded and then pulled back a curtain to reveal a door that led outside.

"Thank ye." Isobel dashed out and around to the front of the building then crossed the street. She stepped into the crowded tavern.

After walking over to Alex's table, she plopped down to catch her breath. Before she could say a word, he started, "What the hell are ye doing in Edinburgh?"

She blinked. She'd heard him use that tone with many men, but never her. What had she done to deserve his ire? "It doesnae matter. What I need to ken is where to find Torsten Campbell. He kens who I am, and if I dinnae take care of him, he may try to get to me through someone else."

"Ye are supposed to be married and safe in Skye."

How had he known that? Her shoulders drooped because she hadn't been the one to give him the news. Had he been keeping tabs on her? Of course he had. Alex Gordon always knew what everyone was doing.

"Well, ye look bonny. He seems to be taking care of ye.

Except that he's letting ye walk the streets out in the open where anyone can see you."

The last thing she wanted was a lecture from her supposed ally. "He thinks if everyone believes me a proper lady, suspicion will no' land on me."

"Aye. Ye fit the part nicely." He smiled at her. "Ye should be with yer husband."

A vise clasped around the meat of her arm, digging in like a falcon's talons around its prey. It pulled her up, and she was drawn into a hard, warm wall of muscle. Alex jumped up and glared at the man behind her.

"Aye, she is married." Grant's smooth voice pulsed through the air, carrying with it a fierce bite she'd not yet heard from him.

Alex's shoulders relaxed somewhat, but her husband's did not.

"Ye must be Grant MacDonald. I'm Alexander Gordon." When Grant made no move to return the greeting, Alex eased back into the chair.

"Sit." The order was ground into her ear as the hand clenched around her loosened. She did and her husband followed into the seat beside her, his hand coming to rest possessively on her leg.

Alex looked as if he were going to laugh, but Isobel saw nothing humorous in the situation. Her husband was acting like he was jealous, but that wasn't possible. He hated her.

"Why is it, wife, that I find ye sneaking into a tavern to meet another man?" Grant's ire was directed at her, but his glare never wavered from the man across the table.

"Nae," she rushed in, "'tis no' like that." She glanced to Alex, who unbelievably looked like he approved of Grant's question. His eyebrows rose and he quirked his head waiting for her response.

"I thought he would ken where to find Torsten Campbell,"

she blurted out, afraid of her husband for the first time, especially now that Alex was in agreement with him.

"And does he?"

"Why would ye two be looking for a Campbell?" Alex's eyes darkened, and his loose, aloof posture turned threatening, showing Grant why he was feared by so many.

"He kens who I am. In the skirmish where I was hurt and ye sent me away, 'twas Torsten Campbell who did it and he recognized me. We have to find him before he tells Argyll."

Alex ignored her and pinned Grant with the next words. "Ye have to get her back to Skye. She is no' safe here. There are Campbells everywhere."

"I agree. She was to be guarded, but I find her here with ye." Grant's accusing glare clung to Alex a moment and then shot to her.

Boyd came rushing up to the table. "How the hell did ye get in here, lass?" He sounded almost as angry as the other men.

"Take her back to the inn and dinnae let her out of yer sight. I'll be back shortly," Grant said. The rage pulsing in Grant's eyes warned her it was not the time to protest his orders. She glanced to Alex for support.

"Go, Isobel. 'Tis best if ye listen to yer husband," Alex's deep voice cut in—he didn't want her there, either.

She stood. "How's Stew?" She had to know how the lad was faring without her there to keep him safe.

"A Macnab man said they were in need of help in their stables. I sent him to live with them." Alex didn't take his regard from Grant as he spoke.

She smiled and relief flooded her. Then she followed Boyd and wondered if both men still at the table would make it out of the tavern standing.

• • •

Staring at the man on the other side of the table, Grant clenched his fists. He kept them at his sides, ready to attack while he tried to erect a calm facade. He wasn't feeling it. "Why is it I find my wife here with ye?"

"There has never been anything between us other than my concern for her well-being." Alex leaned in, serious, and Grant almost believed him, but the shock of finding Isobel here was still raw.

"And do ye think 'tis wise for her to be meeting with ye? How did ye ken she was in Edinburgh?"

"I didnae ken she was here. I passed her on the streets and told her where I would be. 'Tis just a coincidence."

"Then we need to be certain it doesnae happen again. She is done with that life." How many times did he have to tell people that? Luckily, the man nodded, or he might have jumped over the table and attacked. He felt anything but rational.

"She never should have been in it in the first place." Alex's words soothed him slightly and he was thankful the man seemed to have some sense.

"She looks lovely, by the way. I almost didn't recognize her. How did ye get her to put on a gown?" Alex laughed, but the question riled him.

The notion that another man might know her more intimately stung. She had been a maiden when they'd married, but she obviously had some bond with this man. One that led her to steal away from his men and meet clandestinely in a tavern. It was only by luck Parliament had dismissed early, and he'd been on the street to catch a glimpse of Isobel walking in.

"'Tis important she is no' recognized." Grant tried to keep some of the bite out of the words, but the man should realize by meeting her here it put Isobel in danger, and the rebel leader needed to know he wasn't going to allow it again.

Alex nodded. "Aye, and I think yer plan is a good one. The more she is seen about as the lady she is, the less likely anyone is to believe she ever fought with us."

A barmaid approached, but Grant shooed her away. *Damn*, he was trying to meet with Parliament and didn't need to be seen with this man, either.

"Why did she join yer group?"

"She came for her own reasons and then stayed to protect Stew. She is no' like the rest of us."

"How is that?" Folding his arms across the table, he leaned in.

"She was no' fighting for the cause. There is something deeper she never shared with me." Alex shrugged.

"Who's Stew?"

"A lad we saved after his family had been slaughtered by some of Argyll's men. He had no home, so he stayed by my side. Isobel watched over him."

Grant didn't have time to think over Isobel's actions as he faced down the man in front of him, but he was thankful to hear Stew wasn't another man after her affections.

"Do ye ken where we can find this Torsten Campbell?"

"Aye. I'd go after him myself, if there wasnae some business I have to look into."

"Where? I want to make him an offer."

"He is a Campbell. Ye cannae trust him." The man lounged back in his chair, lifting his cup and taking a swig of what was probably ale. "Ye shouldnae go after him. Meet him on neutral ground, but prepare to be ambushed. I've no' heard nice things about him."

"Can ye get word to him?"

"Aye. But under one condition. Ye keep Isobel away from him and whatever men he brings. She will want to try to take them out on her own, but I'm certain she couldnae face them all."

"Agreed. I dinnae want her anywhere near danger or the life ye have helped her lead. She is done with this business."

"I hope so. She deserves better. Keep her on Skye where she'll be safe."

Realizing Alex and he wanted the same thing for Isobel, he relaxed. How was it Grant had so much in common with a criminal?

After discussing a plan to get Torsten Campbell to the northern part of the Cameron lands, across the water from Skye, Grant gave Alex the letter he'd penned, confident he had an ally in Alex Gordon, at least where Isobel's safely was concerned. After his initial shock of finding them here, he was surprised he was coming to respect the man. He'd never thought it possible, but here he was discussing his wife, Scotland, and religion with the infamous head of the Royalist Resistance. And it turned out, although their methods were different, they wanted many of the same things.

Satisfied, Grant pushed back from the table with one thing in mind—it was time to inform Isobel he would not tolerate clandestine meetings with other men or her participation in Royalist Resistance activities.

Chapter Fourteen

Grant took a deep, calming breath before inserting the key and unlocking the door to the room they had rented. Isobel paced like a caged bird looking for an escape.

"Yer behavior is unacceptable," he said.

She stopped and peered at him with eyes as sharp as the sword she probably wished to use on his throat. "Ye have nae right to lock me in this room."

"I do and I will as long as ye cause trouble, wife." He had to admit despite the malice that dripped from his tone, he was doing a fine job of not losing his temper.

Sighing, she pivoted and stomped toward the window, keeping her back to him; the only sign of any remorse was her silence.

"Why did ye feel it necessary to sneak away from my men and put yerself in danger?"

Twirling back to face him, she blurted, "I didnae put myself at risk."

"Aye, ye did. There will be no more meetings with anyone from that rebel group. Ye are done with them."

"I was just trying to find out how to get to the Campbell man. I cannae leave until I've taken out that threat."

"Ye will let me deal with him, and I will never catch ye somewhere alone with another man."

Damn, he was jealous. He'd expected her to do something foolish on this trip—stab someone, cause a fight, obstruct Parliament, but those would have been expected. It had bothered him, no, it had *hurt*, to see her sitting alone at a table with a man who was not him.

After crossing the room, he coiled his arm around her and drew her into his body. "Ye belong to me." His lips crashed down on hers, hoping to wash away the memory of any other man who might have been lucky enough to kiss her, wanting to make her forget the rebels she'd fought with and the man who had taken her in and kept her safe. He wanted to be the one to protect her.

Isobel's mouth opened to him, and his tongue swirled in as her body melted into his. Sighing, she slid her hands around his sides and held onto him as if she trusted him to guard her. He could never give her his heart, but she was his and he'd never let anything happen to her—this threat had to be taken care of. Hopefully, Torsten Campbell was a man of reason, but he'd take Alexander Gordon's advice and stay vigilant.

He drew her in closer, increasing the urgency of their embrace. Just the thought of something happening to her crushed his chest.

Before long, they were a tangled heap of naked limbs, sated and calm. Rolling off of Isobel, he came to rest on his elbow beside her and traced his fingers along her still fevered flesh.

Her gaze met his. "How did it go at the meeting?"

"I didnae get the chance to speak. They ended early today."

"I'm sorry. I ken how important this is for ye." She seemed sincere. Her words fueled a hope that maybe she could change, and that he had the chance to tame her savage side. If he could do that, surely he could sway Parliament.

"I'll try again tomorrow, but I was hoping we'd be on our way back to Skye soon."

"Do ye miss it, then?"

"Aye, I do, and one day 'twill be a home ye miss, too."

A sad smile spread across her lips.

"I bet even now, yer cat is wondering where ye are and when ye are coming home."

"Surely by now it's found a new home."

"And why would anyone give up getting to wake with ye in their bed?" He trailed his fingers in circles on her arm.

"Do I please ye?"

"Aye." Why would she think she didn't?

Her gaze shifted away as color rose to her cheeks. "I am happy I do so," she said.

As confident as the lass was in battle, she had a side of her that was timid. It was an odd contradiction, and he felt honored she let him see her vulnerable side. But why was it there? Had someone hurt her in the past?

"I have something for ye." He reached for the cloth that sat on the nightstand.

"I dinnae need anything else." She sat up and pulled the covers to cover her chest.

"But I want ye to have this. I bought it before I went to Parliament." Although he'd not been eager at the beginning of their relationship, he was pleased with her for a wife.

He unwrapped the cloth to reveal a band with a small, square-cut blue stone in the middle. Taking her left hand, he slid it onto her finger. Some odd emotion washed over him; it just felt right.

The fit was perfect, and it looked like he'd chosen wisely.

Isobel's hand shook as she inspected it, and he thought her eyes misted.

"Thank ye," she said as she dropped the blankets and wrapped her arms around him. It was the first time they'd held each other that had nothing to do with bed play, and he liked it. He returned the embrace.

For the first time since seeing her face at the end of the aisle in the chapel where they'd been wed, he thought they had a chance at making their marriage about something more than bed play for producing heirs.

They declined taking the late meal with the others in the common area. On top of keeping her hidden away, Grant wanted to keep her naked and in his arms.

The next morning, he climbed from the bed and dressed to make his way to the Kirk. He wished for nothing more than to finish his mission and return home. He didn't want to hear men talking ceaselessly of how Scotland was better off with one religion, unified under what they believed was the right way for everyone to worship. He believed all men and women should be allowed to make their own choices.

After thoroughly kissing his wife, he left her some coins and bounded downstairs to talk to his men. "Take care and dinnae let her out of yer sights today."

"What if she wants to try on a garment or two?" Ian gave him a sly smile and continued, "I'd be more than happy to accompany her."

"If she wishes to try something on, it can be done when I return. Better yet, if ye can talk them into coming back here and doing something where she's no' out in the public eye, do it. Maybe get her and Annis a deck of cards to play up in the room."

"I'll try, but I dinnae ken if she'll go for it."

"Try anyway." And he trudged down the street, hoping for the best.

Hours later, he made his way back to the inn. The Scottish Parliament had denied the Royalist clans' demand they dissolve any agreement with the English Parliament against the king. Scotland was going to sign the Solemn League and Covenant and become involved in the English Civil War.

He wished for nothing more than to collect his wife and friends and head home.

Just as he breached the door of the establishment, Boyd and Owen came trotting down the stairs, Boyd's face flushed red with exertion as if the man had been running.

Dread pierced his lungs when he realized something was wrong.

• • •

After Grant left, Annis was again waiting to tie Isobel up in an overly full, deep-blue confection of layers. Today, she didn't bother looking in the mirror. Grant seemed to find her attractive, and he was the only one who mattered. She had to admit, she felt more feminine in the garments and was becoming more tolerant of the restrictive nature of the bindings.

She stared down at the lovely ring her husband had given her and wondered if he knew the color of the stone matched his bonny eyes. She'd not expected such a gift from him, and she hoped it was because he had changed his mind and was now pleased with her as a wife. Perhaps he no longer hated her. As she stroked the token from Grant, for the first time, she acknowledged, she wanted to be a wife he would be proud to have.

As Annis and she left the room to break their fast below, she scooped up the coins her husband had given her. She'd explained how she'd been able to sneak away from his men and had asked if she could return to make good on her word to the shopkeeper. Grant had seemed pleased she wanted to be honorable, as if he'd not expected it of her.

That was the other thing—she'd promised him she would stay out of trouble today and she intended not to disappoint him. It had been more than just anger she'd seen in his eyes yesterday. Although she could be wrong, it almost looked as if hurt was hidden in the sapphire depths of his gaze.

After buying stockings, she easily persuaded the men to return to the inn to share a meal and drop off her purchases. It was harder convincing them to get out of the city— Edinburgh was beautiful, but she wasn't accustomed to the closed-in places and crowded city streets. Fresh air would do her good and staying away from the crowds would prevent her from doing something that might upset Grant.

In the end, Boyd and Ian agreed to escort Annis and her, while Owen stayed behind to rest because he had taken the night watch. Her husband was vigilant about seeing to the group's safety. She smiled at the thought.

"Let's go up there." Isobel pointed to a tall hill. Really, it could have been a mountain, but she didn't care. It was the first time she'd been able to truly breathe since coming to the city.

"That's a long climb."

"We dinnae have to go all the way to the top. Just high enough to look down on the city and the castle."

The group was about half an hour into the trek when they rounded the side of the hill and lost their view of the city. They picked up the pace, since they were no longer afforded the view, but to her, this side with its view of the country was just as beautiful. She could see for miles and she understood why it was rumored to be one of the possible locations of the legendary Camelot.

Annis cried out behind her. Isobel spun and found her maid had collapsed to the ground and was reaching for her foot.

"I think I twisted my ankle." The girl winced.

"Och. Let me have a look at it." Kneeling down, she gently took her maid's foot into her hand. It was already swelling.

"It hurts." Annis inhaled sharply.

"Aye, I imagine it does." The size of it worried her. Annis started to rise, but she placed a hand on the lass's shoulder. "Nae, keep off of it."

Standing, she glanced at Ian, the bigger of the two men. "Can ye get her on that rock so she is comfortable? I think our walk may be over."

"Do ye want me to just carry her back?"

"Nae 'twill take too long and 'twill risk knocking her foot into something and making it worse." She regretted asking them to take the smaller path that had been less traveled.

The two men exchanged looks, then Ian stepped forward to inspect Annis's injury. They were apparently trying to decide what Grant would say if they split up or, worse yet, whether or not she was faking it in an attempt to try something foolish. "I amnae going anywhere. I swear."

Their gazes studied her then returned to each other. Ian nodded his approval.

"I'll go get a horse so she can ride back," Boyd said.

"That will do. We'll just wait here until ye return," she said.

As Boyd took off running back down the trail, she focused on Annis. Diverting her from thinking about the pain, she asked, "What is the first thing ye will do when we get back home?"

"That's easy. I'll go visit Artie at the bakery." Annis tried to hide it, but Isobel could hear the pain in the maid's voice.

"Who's Artie?" She'd not heard this name before.

"He's the man I want to marry."

Suddenly, Isobel felt guilty about pushing the girl away

and not getting to know her.

The discussion continued until Annis adjusted on the rock and then winced.

"Try to keep it propped up. I've heard it helps with the swelling."

"Have ye spent time with healers?"

"I've just helped escort hurt men to see them. 'Twas one of the tasks I was assigned when the leader of the Resistance didnae want me involved in a conflict."

Despite all the skirmishes she'd been rumored to be involved in, mostly she'd been in charge of getting the wounded to safety. She had never complained, because she had been there to protect those who could not take care of themselves.

The first time she'd encountered the Resistance was after she'd seen smoke coming from a MacLean family farm. Upon arriving at the scene, she discovered that everyone had been murdered by a group of Covenanters traveling through her clan's lands. She attempted to track the villains, but found Alex's band along the way. She saw the chance meeting as her opportunity to finally help others.

Because of what had happened when her maid deserted her, her brothers had let her train with them in the lists. Alex saw that she was capable of defending herself when they'd been attacked by the same group who had murdered her clansmen. He'd not argued when she'd said she wanted to stay and help. Then she remained to help guard Stew. But now the lad had a home and it appeared she did as well, there was no reason to rejoin the Resistance. She had Annis to look after now.

"So ye didnae fight in every battle?"

"Nae, but I've run a blade through my share of men. Only when I needed to, and it was always to keep others safe. But I did practice every day, so I was quite handy with a sword."

"And who was it ye were there to protect?"

Unbidden, a vision of her last maid popped into her head. Ignoring the question, she gingerly probed the swelling and Annis winced. "Och, look at it, Annis. 'Tis twice the size it should be. Ye may no' be walking for a while."

A loud *thwack* sounded behind her, and she turned to see what Ian had done. Foot twisting in her skirt, she lost her balance and fell to her hands and knees. Pain shot through her palms where rocks dug into her hands, but it was nothing compared to the fear that pierced her heart when she saw Ian sprawled on the ground in front of her, blood escaping from an injury on his head.

Chapter Fifteen

Grant studied his friends' worried faces as they rushed toward him. He clenched his fists. What had his wife done now? "Where is Isobel?"

Boyd and Owen glanced at each other before Boyd turned to him, looking resigned. "They're on the hill." His man pointed toward the large mound overlooking the town.

"What the hell is she doing there?" His temper rose. The last thing he wanted after the day he'd had was to have to track down his wife and get her out of some sort of trouble.

"'Tis no' anything too bad. We went for a walk. Annis fell and twisted her foot. I came back to get the horses so she wouldnae have to walk on it."

"All right then. Let's go get them."

"Were ye able to speak today?" Owen asked.

"'Tis no' good news. I can tell by yer face." Boyd frowned.

"They didnae want to listen to any of us." He debated whether the men needed to know the rest and decided it would be for the best to be open. "They even tried to coerce me into signing the Covenants for the MacDonald clan."

"Nae." He could hear the sympathy and disappointment in Owen's voice. Out of all the MacDonald men, Owen understood his quest for peace the most.

"For a few moments, I thought they were going to arrest all of the Royalists until our clans agreed to sign."

"What did ye do?" Owen asked.

"The only thing I could—I told them no."

"Och." Boyd shook his head.

"'Tis a shame they wouldnae even listen," Owen said.

"At least there is the meeting tomorrow with the other Royalist clans. Perhaps we can come up with a way to handle the repercussions of Parliament's decision and how it will change life in the Highlands."

The men nodded.

"Will Annis be all right?"

"Aye, 'tis just a twisted ankle. She'll be sore for a while, but shouldnae have trouble as long as she stays off it."

"I'll be down shortly. I want to grab my sword." Grant rushed up the steps to retrieve his weapon since he hadn't been allowed to carry it into Parliament.

A short while later, they rode out of the main city, and he felt like he could finally breathe again. Clouds had started moving in, and he could see rain off in the distance. It would probably catch up to them soon. Kicking his heel into the side of his mount, he spurred his horse on and they started a measured trot toward the hill to retrieve his Isobel.

• • •

From her position on the ground, Isobel peered at the bandits. Fear reigned for only a moment as they studied Annis and her as if they were beggars given admittance to the king's Christmas feast. They wore their weapons openly, showing they wouldn't hesitate to harm anyone who stood between them and what they were after.

"Look what we have here," the largest of the three said as he stepped forward, giving her the impression he might be the leader of the group. His protruding lower lip vibrated and he smacked it against the upper one. He reminded her of a dog with loose jowls.

The comment was intended to strike fear. It worked. Despite her experience, a shiver ran across her skin. She didn't have a weapon, and the sheer size and number of men was menacing. When faced with a confrontation, she'd always had warriors with the Royalist Resistance at her side. With Annis injured and Ian possibly dead, she was on her own.

Her gaze skimmed the multitude of arms the crew had strapped to their bodies. A quick scan told her it wouldn't be possible to lift one before they could attack. They were all holstered well.

Her best bet would be to remove the claymore strapped to Ian's back, but she would need a distraction to reach it without notice.

She started to stand, but a second one spoke. "Nae, lass. Dinnae move." He had blond hair, a long nose, and red skin blotched from too much time in the sun.

Her stomach knotted. Her gaze drifted to Ian's sword again.

"Dinnae count on him, lass. He willnae be getting up for some time." The blond man laughed.

She gulped. She'd have to be more furtive with her gaze or they might think her a danger. Her only advantage was that she appeared defenseless. Best not to let them know different.

"Check the man to see what he's got on him." The leader nodded to the others and one started patting around Ian's plaid.

Annis gasped and the men chuckled, a symphony of clanging tones and cruel intentions of men who had no moral intent. Dread seized her as it had on that day long ago and she almost froze with the fear, but she pushed it back and remained calm.

Even if she didn't survive this, she had to save Annis and Ian, if he was still alive.

Isobel stood.

"Hey now, lass. He said stay down," the drill master of the motley lot clipped.

She glanced at her gown, wondering how she would take all three in this horrid confection of a confining garment. But she was thankful she'd chosen her most casual dress for their hike, the one that allowed the most movement. At least she looked sweet, innocent, and non-threatening trussed up like a fancy cake. It might buy her time if she appeared docile, but she would not get back down. In that position, she was too vulnerable.

"My knees and hands are hurt." Her voice shook with the anger bubbling up, although she hoped it came across as fear. Let them think her weak.

"'Twill nae be the only part of ye hurting for long," the leader laughed, then the blond, scarred man snorted.

If these men had their way, Annis and she might not live through the next few minutes. She'd run across ruthless bandits who stole for a living, and these men seemed desperate enough to be outlaws of the worst sort. They would be swift in their work and show no mercy before fleeing to avoid capture.

The third man, who had not yet spoken, studied Annis like a pastry left out on a table. He had one eye black from a recent altercation and an ominous red scar zagging across his face. His matted red hair gave him a crazed appearance. He was the one she worried about, not because he was the most dangerous, but because of whom he had set his sights on. Isobel would do everything she could to guard Annis's honor and deliver her safely back home to her love.

She would not fail this time, even if it cost her life.

At her distraction, the leader bolted forward and fisted her hair. He forced her head to tilt up to eyes tinged with excitement and madness. "Give me that trinket on yer finger. 'Twill fetch a hefty coin or two."

"Nae. Please. 'Twas given to me by my husband." Somehow, she had to buy time.

"Back on yer knees, wench, and give me that ring." The leader shoved her down. She winced, rocks again digging into her knees despite the padding of her skirts. The blond stepped forward, a sick grin plastered on his face. He licked his lips.

"Red, check the lass on the rock. We dinnae have much time," the leader barked to the scarred one.

Annis. Nae!

"The other man who was with us. He went for the rest of our party. They will be right back." It was a lie, but desperation and urgency beat like a drum through her veins. She had to do something, because these brutes had no intention of leaving witnesses to their theft.

"Be quick about it." The leader released her head, pushing her toward the blond, who started for her hand. She let the movement steer her closer to Ian's prone body.

Cries from behind her pierced her ears. "Nae, let go of me."

The sound of a hand hitting soft flesh smacked her senses then Annis gasped in pain.

Nae. No' again.

Sounds of today mingled with those of the past, splitting her mind in two with fear and helplessness. She squared her shoulders. Taking a deep breath, she vowed this would not end like the last time or worse.

She jerked away from the man in front of her. He growled and unstrapped a knife at his waist.

The claymore was still secured to Ian's body. While the blond was distracted, she feigned falling forward and unbelted the sword. But before she could unsheathe it, the brute grabbed her hair, yanking her out of reach of the weapon.

Her hand swept the ground and clamped around a large stone. Praying God would be with her, she smashed the rock into her captor's knee. He yelled out, but didn't let go, so she couldn't reach the sword.

"Ye shouldnae have done that, wench." The grip on her hair eased just before pain exploded in the back of her skull. She fell onto her cheek, gravel piercing her skin, her head humming. Luckily, she landed within reach of the claymore.

A boot dug into her hip as the man spat at her. Annis screamed again.

Pushing away the pain, she grabbed the hilt and drew the sword. She rolled away from Ian's body and jumped to her feet. She wobbled, more from the blow to her head than the unfamiliar weapon—she'd practiced with claymores to improve her strength and agility, but had never had to use one in battle, preferring to use a short sword for its lighter weight.

Her gaze swung wildly from one man to the next. Even Red had stopped his assault on Annis to appraise her.

"Ye cannae use that, lass. It weighs more than ye do." The blond looked amused.

"Leave now, or I'll be forced to kill ye all."

They stilled for a moment, then the leader started laughing. The other two followed with snickers, but she wasn't fooled. Red left Annis's side and moved nearer to disarm her.

She lifted the blade into a defensive stance, and the men's amusement turned to caution. Even if they thought her a weak woman, they respected the power in her hands and possibly saw now that she was no novice.

"Put it down now, lass," the leader coaxed, trying to sound reassuring.

"Leave us be." She aimed the sword toward Red, who had gotten closer to her than she liked. The man threw up his hands and retreated slightly. From the corner of her eye, she saw the blond remove the claymore from his back and start to slide it from its sheath.

"Put it down before we're forced to hurt ye. It would be a shame to cut ye down before we're done with ye." Nothing in Red's statement reassured her.

Striking before they realized what she was capable of, she went for the immediate threat: Red. She sliced the blade through the air in a swift motion, landing a deep, piercing blow that cut through his arm and side.

Crimson ran from the wound as the redhead dropped his weapon and reached for the injury. Shock registered in his cold eyes as he realized she'd dealt him a fatal blow. Stumbling back, his gaze drifted to the two men left standing. Hers did the same.

The leader seemed to be frightened, while the large blond man who had been after her ring appeared to smile, a maniacal visage that curdled her blood and had her taking a step back. She'd seen men like him before, ones who were excited by battle and thrived on the misery of pain they inflicted on others. She'd never had to defend herself against one. This would be harder than any battle she'd fought before.

And if the blond got his hands on her maid, he would destroy the lass. She'd tried to not let herself care for the girl, but Annis had grown on her.

Isobel wouldn't repeat the past.

She wouldn't let Annis get hurt.

That was what kept her rooted to the spot and pulling Ian's sword up for another round. But the blond didn't seem interested in the sweet maid, his eyes were lit with excitement and blood lust. His dilated gaze was intent on her as she lifted a blade similar in size to the one she held.

He smiled and lunged. Isobel pulled up just in time to block his blow, the clang of metal hitting metal rent through the air then a screech sounded as one blade slid off the other. The force of the blow had her stumbling backward. Vibrations jolted into her elbows and up to her shoulders. Numbness spread through her limbs, and she fought against fatigue to pull her weapon back up.

"Cam," shouted the leader, but the man eyeing her kept his focus on her, ready to rip her apart.

"Cam. Dinnae kill 'er. I want to make her suffer for what she did to Red."

Knowing she was outmatched, she wanted to run. The steel in her arms became heavier with each second. If only she had her short sword and wasn't wearing this impractical dress. The only thing she had going for her was his strikes were clumsy, and the leader now wanted her alive.

The beast struck again and under the force, her weapon flew from her hands, clanging to the ground and out of reach.

The monster dropped his sword and dove for her, knocking her to the ground. Air whooshed from her lungs as her back hit solid earth and rocks. Cam landed on top of her.

She struggled, but he grabbed her hands and brought them up over her head. She resisted, but he laughed.

"I like a wench with some fire in her." He ground his hips into her pelvis. A rock dug into her lower back, and real fear snaked its way into her heart. This was the man to be feared, not the leader. Cam was the one really in control of the group.

He pulled her hands together and attempted to lock them under one of his large ones but she was able to slip one free and project it toward his eyes. He caught her before she could connect. Laughing, he slammed her arm back to the ground. If she let him pin both of her wrists with one hand she'd be done. He attempted, but she slipped through his grasp again.

The flat side of his palm slapped her cheek, sending her face sideways and stunning her for a moment. She recovered quickly and reached for the dagger strapped to the brute's side. It released easily.

Tilting the blade up, she pushed and punctured his side, but instead of causing injury, it seemed to multiply his fury as his hand returned to her face, the stinging reaching all the way from her cheek to her ear. It burned. He growled and pushed back from her, attempting to get at the knife still lodged in his side. Blood oozed from the wound and onto her gown.

They both glanced at the spot, then his rage rose up again and she knew if she didn't strike first, it was over. He pulled back with a closed fist, but before he could connect, she grabbed the hilt, withdrew it, and plunged the blade again. This time, she angled the knife into his stomach and up toward his ribs.

He roared. It was a feral sound that invaded her ears and left her nerves quavering as ice pumped through her whole body. He lifted his fist again, but before he struck, he was knocked sideways. The pressure on her chest eased, and she glanced up to see Annis standing above her with a large club.

The leader's hands wrapped around her maid and pulled the girl back, knocking the large stick to the ground. Words spilled from the maid's lips as she tilted up to shout toward the city. "Help!"

But no help was coming. The pressure returned and she couldn't breathe, could barely move as the blond reemerged to pin her chest with a meaty arm. He glanced down to inspect his wound. She grabbed the dirk and pulled. After it slid free, she drove it back in to the hilt.

A stunned moment later, the brute fell on top of her and began moaning. She twisted and he curled enough that she was able to push him off, but in doing so, the knife remained buried in his side. She crawled away, coughing and trying to fill her lungs, then scurried out of his reach in case he rose to attack again.

Her hands shook and her gaze drifted down to steady

them, but when she took in the blood covering one, she trembled harder. Tearing her attention away, she focused on the threat again. He still writhed on the ground and looked as if he were trying to stand. She turned to collect Annis and run for the city.

Freezing when the leader blocked her way, she realized her mistake. In the scuffle, she'd only been concerned with the blond and Annis, forgetting there was still another danger present. Before she could act, the man had pulled a dag from his belt and aimed it straight at her. She'd seen what happened to men when one of the lead shots from those pistols entered a body. It was as deadly as a sword or dirk. And it hit too quick for someone to outmaneuver.

She backed away, thankful the man's focus was all on her and he'd forgotten about the maid. Relief filled her lungs as Ian began to stand, but he stumbled and went back down on a knee. She had to keep the man's attention from turning that way.

"Ye cannae blame me for defending myself."

"Who are ye and how did ye just take out two men?"

Hell, if he figured out the truth, it would be better if he shot her. She couldn't go to Argyll, because she'd be tortured for all she knew of the Royalist Resistance. Letting her gaze shift to Ian for only a second, she noticed he was having trouble and wouldn't make it in time to help.

Then she spared a glance for the man who still thrashed on the packed earth and rocks with Ian's sword just a few feet away. Her gaze returned to the leader, but she inched toward the weapon as she held her hands up, praying she could be swift and he had a bad aim.

She tried not to let the fear show on her face as she saw Annis limp toward the man, a rock in hand. There was no way to tell the lass to stop without giving her or Ian away. Suddenly, her maid was hurling the stone at the man, hitting him squarely on the back of his head. He jerked left and his pistol fired, the lead shot hitting the packed earth and scattering debris into the air, splattering on her skirts.

The man twisted around to move toward Annis as she ran. It gave Isobel just enough time to retrieve the sword and bring it back to an offensive position, her arms now shaking from fatigue.

"Halt," she ordered before the man could reach her maid. Pivoting back toward her, the man started forward, missing that Ian was now on his feet.

"Now, lass. I think I'll be on my way and leave ye ladies alone." The placating tone belied the anger she saw swirling in his cold, dead eyes. He crept forward, one small measured step at a time, holding out his hands as if he meant her no harm, but she saw the twitch on the hand nearest the dirk still strapped to his side.

"Halt." But he kept coming toward her. Somewhere in the back of her head she thought she heard hoofbeats pound, but it could have been her heart, and she couldn't take her eyes away from the man long enough to look.

"Ye wouldnae hurt a defenseless man," he yelled out for the benefit of whoever was coming around the bend on horseback. His hand dipped and grasped the knife. He lunged forward, but she was quicker. Coming down, she sliced across the man's neck. The blow was not enough to knock him off balance, but she'd nicked the crucial spot on the tender flesh. Life spilled from his veins.

Alex had taught her the killing move, but she'd never had to strike someone there until now.

The man dropped his knife, collapsing to the ground. Confident he was no longer a threat, she took a deep breath. She let her gaze slide up to check on Ian and Annis. But the sight that greeted her was the steely fury-filled gaze of her husband.

Chapter Sixteen

After checking to ensure the men his wife had killed were truly dead, Grant found one still writhing as if he had some fight left in him. Anger pierced his chest at the necessity, but he sank a dirk into the man's back. It didn't look likely the injured bandit would live, but if the man made it back to Edinburgh, he would be able to identify Isobel and put his clan in danger.

Damn her. She had a knack for finding trouble. Had she gone out in search of Torsten? Just when he was starting to think she had a softer side and he could live without constant fear of something happening to her, she proved him wrong.

When he got Isobel back to Skye, he'd keep her locked away from any weapons, perhaps even people. He wanted to take the time to ask Ian what had happened, but they couldn't afford it—they had to get out of here before they were discovered.

"We have to go." His gaze shifted around the group, assessing injuries while trying to determine how they could make it back to the inn undetected.

"What do we do with them?" Boyd came up next to him.

"Pull them to the side and try to hide them under the brush. Maybe that will give us enough time to get to safety."

His gaze shifted to Isobel, who had dropped the claymore she'd wielded with the precision of any Highland warrior. She stared at him as if she could see through him. Her hands still trembled with rage or whatever came over her when she assaulted people. Her clothes were dirty and dappled with blood. Panic assailed him that it might be hers, but she gave no indication other than a stilled tongue that she might be injured.

"Move," he ordered the women. "On the horses. We have to go." Annis limped toward her mare, but Isobel remained planted to the ground.

"Now," he thundered, because his words hadn't registered on his wife's face. If he didn't get her out of here before they were discovered, everyone would know of her past. Annis hopped up beside her, took her hand, and steered her toward her beast.

After hiding the bodies, they galloped down the hillside toward the city. Grant stared at the back of his wife's head, but because he'd not yet gotten his temper in check and his hands still trembled at the thought of her being hurt, he made no move to ride up to speak to her. He was thankful she was alive, but afraid he wouldn't like hearing what had happened with the downed men. He had all night to get answers from Isobel.

Ian looked a little uneasy on his steed, tilting toward one side then jerking to the other. Once they returned to the inn, he'd have to seek out a healer to look over his friend's wound.

Taking in the empty expanse on the well-traveled and cleared road behind them, he said, "Boyd, we can slow a bit."

He pulled his steed next to Ian. Owen trotted along on the other side, keeping a close eye on his twin.

"What happened back there?" Grant asked.

"I dinnae ken." Ian's face was drawn and pale. It was obvious he was lucky to have survived.

"Did ye kill any of them?"

"Nae," Ian answered, but closed his eyelids as if he was trying to remember what had happened.

"Then my wife did it all." How had she taken out three men without any assistance?

"When I woke up, there was only one left. 'Twas just before ye showed up. 'Tis nae possible she took them all out on her own."

Upon reaching the stables, he pulled his wife down from her mare and dusted her clothes as she silently watched him. If he stayed near her as they walked in, no one would notice the splatters on her gown.

Boyd carried Annis in. When they reached the top of the stairs, Isobel attempted to follow her maid, but he steered her toward their room. "Nae, this way."

Something akin to panic lit her gaze. "But I have to be certain she is safe." She tugged, but he kept a firm grip.

"Boyd and the others will see to that."

Her gaze shifted from him, back to the maid. "Nae, 'tis no' enough."

"Someone will be standing guard all night." He used all the authority of one who would one day be laird behind his words. The lighting in the hall was dismal, but he thought he detected a gleam of moisture glimmering in her eyes.

Och, it had been a long day, and now he was seeing things. He pushed in the door and tilted his head for her to enter. She gawked at him when he let go and didn't follow her in. "I'll be right back. Dinnae leave this room and bolt the door behind me."

Hoping to convey urgency, he injected anger from today's events and the fear that she'd been hurt into his order. It had been hard enough sneaking her unseen past the innkeeper's eyes—the worst thing she could do was be seen traipsing around the hall.

The only light was from the small window on the other side of the room, but even with the dull glow of the late evening, he thought she trembled. He didn't think he'd been that gruff.

She didn't look like the defiant woman he was accustomed to. She looked scared, and her unfocused stare tugged at his chest. Now that they were back, he wanted to coil his arms around her to reassure himself she remained unharmed, but first, he had to see to the others.

Once he'd walked out, it was several seconds before the bolt fell into place, almost long enough he contemplated ordering her to latch it. After ensuring Owen was in the hall keeping watch, he requested a meal brought to each room, along with a basin of water and rags, and a healer for Ian.

When he returned to the room, he knocked and Isobel opened the door straight away—it was as if she hadn't moved from the spot where she'd stood when she'd locked it.

He sidled past her and lit a candle. "We will have some food shortly. Are ye hungry?"

She hadn't moved and still stood facing the door, trembling.

A memory after his uncle was killed surfaced and slammed into him. He'd been frozen, trapped in some place he hadn't been able to escape, somewhere between fear and disbelief, reliving that moment over and over. The MacDonald healer told him it happened to many men in battle, and it was common for a person who had experienced some kind of suffering to be stuck in a trance.

Had she been hurt today and he'd not realized it?

"Isobel."

She didn't acknowledge him.

He took her trembling hand. She flinched as if burned, but didn't look his way. Inverting her palm, he was shocked by the small punctures that dotted the soft flesh. Anger invaded again, but this time it was toward whatever had caused her such injuries. He spun her to face him. Tears streamed down her cheeks, and something in his chest began to ache.

"She'll leave now. She'll think 'tis my fault." The sheer pain in her expression made him thankful he'd not started the tirade he'd planned about her seeking out Torsten.

"What are ye saying?" He studied her, but her expression didn't change.

"'Tis my fault."

The vacant glaze in her eyes worried him.

"I should have helped. I should have tried harder." The shivering in her hand intensified, and a fresh tear streamed down her cheek.

"Isobel." Taking her upper arms in his hands, he gazed directly at her, hoping it would be enough to draw her from whatever was going on in her head.

It didn't.

"I should have tried harder."

"Isobel." This time he shook her gently and she seemed to settle some, so he drew her to the bed and eased her down on the plush mattress. He was about to sit next to her when someone rapped on the door—servants with both the basin of water and food.

"The healer will be here shortly for yer friend."

"Thank ye," he replied as he backed away, letting the servants enter the room.

"We brought wine, but can bring some ale if ye prefer."

"Nae. 'Tis enough." As they brought the items into the room, he positioned himself in front of Isobel, shielding her from their view.

Realization dawned that he was doing it to protect her in her fragile state and not to hide the evidence of today's events.

Once the servants were gone, he bolted the door, returned to her side, and wondered how he was going to break through to her. It seemed easier to deal with the war-hardened maiden than the delicate lass in front of him now.

. . .

Isobel swam in the murky haze her mind was trapped in. The numbness had lessened slightly, but she still couldn't find her way out.

After removing her slippers and stockings, Grant untied the laces of her bodice then pulled it from her body. Isobel felt as if she could almost breathe again. What had happened to her?

"Stand," he ordered and she obeyed, uncaring except that he seemed so gentle and concerned for her instead of angry.

She wasn't sure where they were, and the ride here was an elusive memory, her thoughts faded like the horizon in a heavy mist.

Grant peeled her skirt from her body and she noticed blood had soaked through to her chemise. Her gaze fixated on it, remembering the fight she'd almost lost. And how she'd almost failed Annis.

The shift was ruined. Proof that she was not worthy of such garments and the attentions other ladies sought. As her husband dropped the material of her gown to the floor, his hands returned to remove the offending shift from her body. He probably thought her a monster.

Grant gathered up the ruined garments and carted them off to a corner, dropping them as if they'd burned him. She could inhale fully now and with the rush of air came the clarity she wanted to be someone he could care for. She no longer wanted to be the scared little lass from the past or the person she'd become.

She hid from the judgment that must be in the depths of his deep brown eyes. The gaze that made a fire burn inside her, made her feel like a woman and made her want to be worthy of him. How could he do all those things to her?

Something cool and wet touched her shoulder. She shivered as Grant slid a rag down her arm, cleaning away the filth of the day. She was mesmerized as he studied her arms then her hands before his attention tilted up.

The condemnation she'd been expecting wasn't there. Concern darkened his gaze and she couldn't turn away from the comfort she found there.

"Are ye feeling better?"

She nodded, not trusting her voice. He gave her a tentative smile, then pivoted to move away. She panicked for a moment, until she realized he was walking back to the basin that had been set on a chair to clean the rag. After rinsing it, he closed the distance between them and started on her other arm.

"What happened today?"

Everything came rushing back. She wanted to run out and check on her maid, but the soothing cloth and Grant's eyes kept her rooted to the spot. *Och*, and she was not clothed. "Annis. Is she all right?"

"Aye. Boyd and Owen are looking out for her. Ian's resting. They'll take shifts."

He continued to drag the soft material against her skin, leaving a trail of gooseflesh along her arms. She winced when he turned her palm up and dabbed at the spots on her hands then drew it up for inspection. She had gouges in her palms where she'd been pushed down on the rocks.

"What happened?"

"I was talking to Annis and heard something." A remembered *thud* sounded in her ears, and her chest tightened. "When I turned, Ian was on the ground and there were men standing over him." She shivered when a memory of the men's feral gazes returned.

Grant lifted her arm and he squinted at something on her side. The tips of his fingers gently dabbed at her ribs, and she inhaled sharply as a piercing pain assailed her. It was the spot where the man had kicked her. It had already started to bruise—it would be sore for quite some time.

"They were going to hurt Annis." She shook her head. "I couldnae let them hurt her."

"Tell me the rest." Grant's breathing had slowed to a measured pace and his eyes darkened. For once, the anger in them did not appear to be directed at her.

"I had nae choice. They threw me down. They were going to take everything then kill us." Bile threatened to rise at what the men had planned for her and the sweet maid. "They were going to hurt Annis."

Grant spun away, his fists clenched, shoulders tight. He strode to her bag and pulled out another shift. She expected him to give it to her, but he pulled her closer to the candlelight, twirling her around and inspecting her side.

"I'll be all right." Her wounds would heal but that all-encompassing feeling of helplessness came flooding back.

He didn't say anything, just continued to scrutinize her in the glow of the flame. "I should have been there," he muttered and kind fingertips caressed her, reminding her she'd been knocked down and pinned between the rocks and that monster.

"Nae, 'twas no' yer doing," she tried to reassure him. It had been her suggestion to go for a walk. He had been trying to secure peace for the Highlands.

"How were ye able to defeat three of them?" Grant's

words cut into her thoughts.

"I only kenned I had to save Annis. 'Twas luck they didnae think me a threat."

"Aye, 'twas." He pulled the shift over her head and she slid her arms through the sleeves. When he eased her around to face him again, he caressed the bruise forming on her cheek. "I willnae let another touch ye again."

His hand slid beneath her chin, tipping it up. He surprised her with a small, simple kiss. His lips erased some of the fear that still ate at her. He only held the contact for a moment, but it was filled with regrets and promises. The connection reminded her of warm sheltered nights before she had discovered the world was cruel.

Pulling back, he smiled and drew her toward the table and the food that had been brought in. "Let's eat."

Grant released her and she eased into the empty chair while he moved the basin. He wiped himself down then carted the tub to the door while she took in his broad shoulders and firm muscles. He returned and sank into the chair across from her.

Two bowls of stew sat on the table, along with some bread, wine, and cheese. She picked at a small piece of bread, popping it into her mouth, but not tasting the morsel. Grant dipped in his spoon and filled it with meat and what looked like potatoes.

Taking a sip of the wine, she savored the rich red liquid as it coated her parched throat and relaxed for the first time since the bandits had attacked them. Setting the goblet down, she pushed back the curls that had escaped her pinned-up tresses. "I must look awful."

"Ye are lovely, even black and blue like ye are."

Warmth crept to her cheeks, and she wondered at how he made her feel like a woman to be desired despite knowing she was not bonny.

She pulled at the pins and let the remainder of her hair fall free, running her fingers through the length of curls, trying to separate the knots that must look hideous. Grant stared at her, looking at ease for the first time in days. And she remembered why he'd been so on edge.

"Did ye have any luck with Parliament?"

"Nae." Shaking his head, he took a long sip of his drink then placed the cup back on the table. "Parliament will sign the Solemn League and Covenant, even almost forced me and the other representatives to sign the damn thing on behalf of the MacDonalds."

"I'm sorry. I ken how much it meant to ye."

"I'm lucky they didnae lock me up until I agreed. Then, I found ye driving a sword through a man."

Afraid she'd see disappointment in his eyes again, she studied the stew and took a sip. The savory soup reached her tongue, but her appetite had not yet returned.

"I'm sorry I thought the worst. I promise I will always listen to yer version first. Finish telling me what happened."

The rest of the meal was spent talking about the incident, and her nerves were still wrangled because although she felt safe, she needed to ensure her maid was all right, too. She jumped up and ran to the door. "Annis, I have to see her."

"Nae. She may be sleeping by now. Let her rest." His fingers clasped hers and squeezed gently. "Come. They willnae let anything happen." He guided her to the bed, but the fear was back and she felt frozen. "Climb in."

He undressed while she slipped under the covers, trying to ignore the aches in her body and the sense of urgency when memories of her maid being attacked flooded her. Swiping at the tears, she cursed herself for being weak and shifted onto her side so her husband couldn't see—she never let herself cry.

How could she trust men to keep Annis safe? It was her

job.

Grant slid in behind her, wrapping his warm arm over her waist, burrowing into her. "Why are ye shaking?"

She couldn't answer because her voice would give her away.

Taking her shoulder, he rolled her to face him. He'd snuffed the candles, but the glow of a summer evening illuminated the room enough she could see his features clearly, which meant he could see her.

"Are ye crying?"

With that, another drop slid down her cheek and she attempted to look away, but he caught her face and drew her gaze to his.

"Och, Isobel. I dinnae wish to see ye hurt and no' be able to do anything about it. 'Tis time ye tell me what troubles ye." His fingers delved into her hair, sending warmth and reassurance to a part of her that hadn't felt secure in years.

Maybe he would understand.

The words would get stuck in her throat, but she took a calming breath to speak about the day her world changed. "I was twelve summers when it happened. It had been raining for days. The storm had finally cleared and it was such a beautiful day." Her mind drifted to the warm sun on her skin, the soft breeze rustling through her hair, and the scent of fresh earth and lilac as they passed through the fields. But, beautiful days were deceiving. "My brother Ross agreed to take Morna and me out to pick berries."

"Who's Morna?"

"She was my maid."

"What happened?"

"Some lass who liked Ross pulled him away, and he left us in the field alone." Her chest tightened as the terror of those moments invaded. "There were two of them. They grabbed us before we kenned what was happening, covered our mouths and dragged us into the woods. They were big men. They were laughing and the one holding Morna took out a knife and cut open her gown. She screamed, but he hit her. I was still pinned by the other one and couldnae do anything." She inhaled, trying to bring air into her chest, trying to finish the tale she'd told no one—it had been Morna who had given Ross and her family the details.

"'Tis okay, Isobel. Ye are here with me now. I'll keep ye safe." Grant cupped her face as his sapphire gaze consoled and comforted.

"Morna was screaming for me to help. I tried. I swear, I tried." She bit her lip.

"'Tis all right, Isobel. I'm here." His tender tone urged her on.

"When the first one was done with her, he looked at the man holding me and said, 'Well what are ye waiting for?' The one holding me answered he didnae want me, he wanted Morna and that I looked like a boy. They both laughed. The first one sat on me while the second one raped her."

Grant's forehead rested on hers, nuzzling back and forth.

"Morna blamed me. When we made it back to Ross and then the castle, she told everyone I didnae help her and she left. She was my best friend and I let her down." She paused, thinking that now her story was told the pressure should ease, but it was still ever-present. "Ye asked me once why I fight."

Grant nodded.

"I do it because I didn't fight hard enough when I needed to and now since I'm stronger, I can. Because I need to protect people who cannae defend themselves."

"Ye were just a child. There was nothing more ye could have done."

"She was my responsibility. I didnae keep her safe, and she left me."

Grant's hand clasped onto hers, the caress tender, without

judgment. "Nae. Ye were in her care and she shouldnae have blamed ye for something ye couldnae control. The blame lies with the men who attacked ye." His gaze took on a dark sheen. "Were they found?"

"I think my brothers found them, but all they ever said was that I would never have to worry about them again. When I fight for the Royalists, it's not because I'm passionate about my religion or the king. 'Tis because I have to protect Stew and my family."

"Ye ken 'twas nae yer fault. Ye were but a child fighting grown men."

"Morna said I didnae do enough."

"She was but a child, too, and ye were the only one she could blame. Ye were both lucky to be left alive."

No one had ever told her it wasn't her fault. She'd kept it locked up inside and only opened the cork and let the anguish out when she had someone to fight. Until now, it had been her only way of dealing with the pain. This was new, and she didn't know how to take his kindness and understanding.

It might make her believe she could trust a man to keep her safe again.

Chapter Seventeen

Grant planted his lips on Isobel's. She was warmth and reassurance, innocence and loyalty, qualities he'd thought her lacking. She'd only been hiding behind the persona she'd adopted. She was a good woman who had been hurt, not the bloodthirsty monster he'd believed her to be.

He wanted to move closer, breathe her in, and revel in who she was. He wanted to protect her and show her that she wasn't alone and he'd never let her be harmed again, and he wanted to show her that she was all woman, his woman. There was nothing boyish about her, but she'd let the words of those arses and unjust accusations taint her perception of who she was.

Deepening the kiss, he let his tongue slide into her mouth to claim his wife, this time feeling a deeper connection with her, a closeness that hadn't existed before. Something more than pleasure spiked in his blood—it was the need to keep her near, keep her safe and make her happy. He wanted to bring back the innocence she'd lost long ago and show her the world could be a good place.

Her tongue twirled with his and her head tilted into the embrace; her answering response told him she was not immune to his touch, that soon, she would be falling into oblivion in his arms. He wanted to do that to her, make her come undone and forget about life outside this room.

Need crashed over him and an urgency to be inside her body overwhelmed him. His fingers forked through her hair. She flinched, and he felt a bump on the back of her head. Remembering all the scrapes and new bruises forming on her hands and back he cursed to himself.

She had taken a real beating today. If she hadn't been able to take care of herself by the time he'd gotten there, she could have been dead.

Freeing her, he pulled back. "Are ye hurting?"

"Aye. Some, but there is nothing to do for it."

His thumb slid across her cheek. He placed his forehead on hers, soaking her in, and said a prayer of thanks to God he'd not lost her today. His lips fell to hers again, savoring slowly and asking for her to give him all.

Matching his strokes, her fingers inched into his curls, massaging, sending tingles through his scalp that begged him to turn into her touch. The pressure in his cock called for him to move faster, to take her and fill his wife with his seed. Somehow, he kept it in check.

Withdrawing, his gaze took in her swollen lips, her dilated eyes, and accelerated rise and fall of her chest beneath her thin shift. Desire darkened her eyes, and the knowledge drove him mad with want.

"Ye dinnae need this." He gently tugged at the last barrier between him and Isobel's tender flesh. "I dinnae want to hurt ye, or I'd rip it from yer body. Take it off."

Her hand dropped from his head, and she pulled up the shift. She shimmied until the material was at her hips, then she sat up and raised the cloth above her head as his gaze rested on her breasts.

His lips caressed the slight dip between her shoulder and the soft mound beneath. Kissing, he worked his way onto her breast and to the peak in the middle. He flicked his tongue across the hard tip as his hand slid up Isobel's side to clasp the other mound, holding it firmly as he suckled the first. She moaned and arched into his touch, driving him to take more, to suck harder, and squeeze the tip of the one he was holding. A soft whimper escaped her throat.

The longing in her gaze mirrored his own hunger. Remembering the bruises still forming on her back he asked, "How are yer knees?"

"Huh?"

"Yer knees. I ken yer back is hurt, but yer knees." Pushing the covers away, he noted they, too, bore scrapes. "Och. I dinnae wish to injure ye." He slid toward the edge of the bed and stood, motioning her to do the same. She had a mildly curious look on her face, but she obeyed.

Once she was on her feet, he guided her toward the chairs. Before sitting, he turned and his gaze drifted over her lean form. It was the body of a woman honed to fight in battles, the figure of the woman who would bear him children. She was lovelier than any lass he'd ever seen, even with scraped knees and the darkening on her face, which foreshadowed the bruising to come.

"Ye are bonny."

Her face held a look of disbelief.

"Dinnae let the past blind ye to what I see so clearly. I wouldnae want to do this if I didnae think ye were the most beautiful lass in all of Scotland."

His lips pressed to her forehead and dotted little caresses all over her warm flesh, down her uninjured cheek to her neck. He stopped to lavish more attention on her sensitive nape. Gently sliding his arm around her waist, he clasped her rear and drew her nearer. His cock ached as the movement pushed him into the smoothness of her belly, and he rotated his hips back and forth, savoring the sensation.

All the while, he didn't let up the assault on the sensitive part of her elegant neck, gliding to where it met her shoulder. He nipped and she leaned into him, a soft sigh deep in her throat. He did it again and she arched, putting more pressure on his staff and driving him to the point of need that spurred him to go faster. He held back.

His free hand stroked and he enjoyed the sleek softness as she tilted into him. He closed his mouth on her again, his teeth skimming her skin as he sucked. She clasped his side and urged him on, tightening her grip on his waist.

He found the soft curls at the apex of what made her all woman and ran his fingers through the silky strands. Isobel's breath hitched. He took his time, wanting to draw out his need, to make the completion, when it came, that much more enjoyable.

Exploring lower, he slid toward her welcoming heat. Spreading her legs slightly, he roamed all the way to the nub at her apex. Gliding his finger over it, he was delighted to feel the moisture there that meant she was ready to take him in. As he circled, she gasped. He could wait no longer.

He eased down into the chair. Taking his cock in his hand, he readied himself. "Come. Put a leg on either side of me."

She inched forward, tentative and unsure. As their centers neared, he let go of himself and pulled her near. She let his lips take from hers. Their tongues swirled in the madness of the moment and the need to sate the hunger that had built and filled him with a need bursting to a level he'd never imagined. He wanted to be one with her, to own her body and her soul, to brand her as his and to show her she would always be safe with him.

Rotating his hips, he rubbed his staff against her pelvis. He wanted to draw out the sensation of ultimate need, because once he was inside her, it would be mere moments before he reached his peak. He was almost ready to burst just with the slightest touch.

Then the pressure was too much to bear. He guided Isobel onto the tip of his manhood. Slowly, savoring the ecstasy of her channel closing in around his shaft, he drew her down, impaling her and making them one. It was like they belonged together, fit perfectly, like the mist on the morning shores of Skye.

Isobel's hands came to rest on his ribs, clinging like a ship moored to the coast. Aye, they were two completely different people, but this was right, this was real. Sudden clarity dawned. He was happy to be tied to this woman, bound to her for the rest of their lives.

Gripping her hips, he thrust, up and into her core, claiming her body. She arched into him, her head lolling back and lips separating on a moan. The sight of her pleasure was more intoxicating than the rush of heat, igniting feelings in him he didn't know he'd been capable of. He'd learned his wife was not the savage he'd believed her to be, but a decent, kindhearted woman who only thought of others.

He ground into her and her hands tightened on his sides as her dilated gaze locked with his, lingering, and showing him her utter abandon. He continued rocking with his hips, clasping one hand onto the back of her neck, pulling her closer. He had to taste her.

The movement drew her body flush with his, her breasts on his chest, the apex of her legs rubbing against his pelvis as he closed his lips on hers. As their embrace deepened, her exotic scent washed over him. Anytime he smelled her, his thoughts would turn to being lost in her arms.

Small mewling noises started in her throat. They turned more urgent and he knew she was about to reach that sweet climax, which pulled him closer to the edge. It was an impossibly high precipice after the fear of her being hurt, the realization he cared for her, and the trust she had placed in him tonight.

Isobel fell into him, every muscle in her body tightening around him, her tongue in his mouth stilling as her breathing changed to gasps of ultimate pleasure. Her sheath clenched around his shaft and pulsated through him. The intensity was almost unbearable. Frenzied currents crashed into him, his seed started to pump into her, and he held on as if he were that ship fighting the raging sea and she was the shore to which he was secured.

She collapsed onto him, her head resting on his shoulder as if she had all the trust in the world in him. And he knew something had shifted for her as well. They were no longer enemies, but had a shared path. In her own way, Isobel had been looking for peace, too. Trying to make amends for something she hadn't needed to and protecting those who were weaker.

They stayed there, sated in each other's arms, for a little while longer. When he felt Isobel starting to relax, he lifted her and carried her to the bed, careful to avoid her injuries. As he placed her on the soft mattress, he caught a glimpse of the red welt on her cheek. It was a reminder he could have lost her today.

A vision of the man he'd grown up with as a brother intruded. The true-life nightmare he'd lived time again in his mind reappeared. It was the vision of the MacLeod laird's son severing his beloved uncle's head from his body. It was a fight his uncle should not have been in, because he had been defending a MacLeod lass who had been abused by the arse. His need to protect the innocent had been the reason trouble had come to the beaches of Skye on that rainy day so long ago.

Until Isobel changed, he couldn't get attached and risk

that heartache again. Despite these newfound emotions, he had to keep his distance. Not until the threat from the Campbell man had been dealt with, and until she gave up her quest to guard everyone.

He'd lost his uncle to the man's need to defend and shelter others. It had crushed him. What would happen to him if he lost Isobel for the same reason?

• • •

As sunlight shone through the window, Isobel woke with a clear head and a conviction she'd done what she could to protect Annis the day before. That didn't, however, stop her from squirming as she fought the urge to jump up and run to check on the lass.

Grant lay beside her, his arm draped over her belly. It was comfortable and becoming a familiar sensation, but she couldn't rise without waking him. She also had a strange desire to stay there and savor the moment, despite the aches plaguing her body. Here, she could study Grant's masculine jawline and his dark lashes that matched the thick black hair she wanted to run her fingers through.

Lulled into a sense of security she'd not felt since she was young, she let her mind wander to a life where battle wasn't an everyday occurrence, where childhood dreams still had a chance of coming true, and people didn't leave.

Once they were on their way back to Skye, she'd feel more confident about Annis's security. There, she could more easily keep an eye on the dangers facing her maid and when she wasn't, she could make sure this baker knew to guard her closely. A trickle of fear spiked in her chest—did the maid believe she'd done enough to protect them yesterday?

She took in Grant's relaxed posture. She'd told him the truth last night, and he'd made her believe she wasn't responsible for what had happened all those years ago. She gulped. She was becoming attached to her husband. She'd been successful for years at keeping others at bay, but now, she'd let herself care about two people—Annis and Grant—who could destroy her if they ever decided they no longer wanted her.

He'd held her last night like she was important to him, like he could come to care for her, and her past would no longer spark outrage in his eyes. She'd never felt so connected with another person. She pushed away the doubt, the fear he would one day rise up and say he no longer wanted her, that she wasn't worthy. It reminded her there was still a threat out there, one greater than she'd ever faced.

Torsten Campbell. She had to get to the man before he could harm Grant.

"Good morning," she said when she realized her husband was watching her.

"Aye, it is. Good morning." He pulled away quickly as if her skin was a hot kettle that had burned him. The chilled air in the room enveloped her and she shivered.

Grant slid from beneath the covers, his features granite and unreadable, the connection from the previous evening gone.

Did he hate her now that he knew her secret?

"We'll take the midday meal with representatives from the other Highland clans today."

Grant's face was solemn. He bore a heavy weight. Though not yet laird, he helped his father shoulder the responsibility of his people. Not only was he born for the role he was destined to inherit, he had the drive and the will to make the tough decisions. He was a born leader.

"To discuss how to proceed, now that Parliament is moving forward with the Solemn League and Covenant?" she questioned.

"Aye. 'Tis going to be a rough road ahead. We'll have to find a way to no' anger Parliament, but still stay true to ourselves. We will do what is necessary to keep the clan safe."

"It may be the best way to keep those ye care about from being harmed." She never thought she'd come to admire the way he tackled hard situations, but she was proud to call him husband.

"We need to pack now, because afterward, we'll be on our way home to Cairntay."

His clan still wouldn't be safe if they didn't eliminate the threat she'd created. "We still have to find Torsten Campbell."

"Nae, we dinnae. I will worry with that."

She sat up, putting her fists on her hips. "Aye, I do." She was sure the authority in her voice was diminished by the lack of clothing she wore. Pulling up the blankets, she covered her breasts. Grant only smirked then retrieved his shirt, pulling it over his head and ignoring her reply.

She rose and ran across the room to collect a fresh shift. After slipping the garment over her head, she faced Grant, who was nearly dressed, and said, "Torsten Campbell is my responsibility. We need to seek him out now. If he comes to MacDonald lands, he may hurt someone in order to get to me."

"I have a plan to deal with the Campbell. Word has been sent to him, and he'll come to me. 'Tis best if ye stay out of it."

"Nae." She put her hands on her hips, but winced at the pain. *Hell*, she hurt everywhere.

"Ye are my wife and will do as I say. After this meeting, we are going home where I can face him on familiar ground, and where I can be certain ye are safe."

"I will take care of it."

"Dinnae challenge me, wife." Grant stalked toward her then stood over her as if he were already laird and ready to do battle to defend his clan. The command in his voice dripped with conviction and power.

Shivering, she spun away and was about to collect her skirts when Grant's arms circled her waist.

His breath was hot on her ear. "For once, let someone shield ye," he pleaded. He nuzzled into the side of her head, inhaling as if he were breathing her in. Then he was slipping out of the room and she was met with a closing door and the certainty that no matter what she said, he would not give.

But she wouldn't, either.

A light rap sounded, followed by the creak of the door. "Good morning," Annis chirped as she hobbled into the room.

A heaviness weighing on her chest lifted. Isobel rushed forward to hug her, relief flooding her when Annis's arms closed around her in return.

"How is yer foot?"

"I'll survive. It only hurts when I put my whole weight on it." The maid giggled.

"Thank you for nae being angry with me."

"Why would I be upset with ye? Ye saved both our lives yesterday. I'll no' be leaving yer side the rest of the journey back."

Isobel's eyes stung with moisture.

"Ye probably saved Ian as well. They would have killed him if he'd woken before he did, because he was in no shape to fight."

"Och, is he all right?"

"A healer came to see to him last night. Said he would mend, but to go easy on the journey." Annis laughed. "I heard him arguing with Owen in the hall this morning. He wanted to take a turn watching the doors, but his brother wouldnae hear of it. Said he was ordered to rest."

Luckily, she was able to convince Annis to fashion a simple braid. Annis hurried to pack while Grant and she were at this meeting. Because Isobel needed to act like a proper lady to prove she was a meek lass, she still had to wear a dress.

As they sat in a private booth in the common area breaking their fast, Grant leaned in and slid something across the table to her. "I think ye should have this."

Lifting his hand, she blinked at his offering. A *sgian-dubh*. The knife was simple, with a hilt made from the smoothed antler of a deer and a blade about five inches long. Perfect for defending oneself or others in close combat. She wanted to jump across the table and plant her lips on his. It was the best gift she had ever received. The straight blade was polished and sharp, ready to defend its wearer against enemies, but what she valued most was the untouchable gift he gave. His trust.

Neither spoke as he reached under the table and took her calf in his hand. Pushing up her skirts, he holstered and secured the knife to her leg, the perfect spot. Easily reachable whether she needed to slice a cut of meat or defend herself in battle. Once safely attached, he pulled down the material of her gown to cover it.

"Thank ye," she managed without choking. He only nodded.

"Are ye ready?"

"Aye." Peace invaded her senses, and something unexpected happened—her heart fluttered. He was trusting her and giving her permission to be who she was. If they weren't rushing out, she'd draw him near and hold him. For the first time in ages, she felt truly safe and understood.

"Boyd is staying to keep watch on Ian and Annis. They should have everything ready to depart upon our return."

Owen met them at the stables where they mounted and rode across the city to meet with the other Royalist lairds at Holyrood Abbey.

Chapter Eighteen

As they reached the Abbey stables, Isobel saw faces she recognized. First was Brodie Cameron. Until recently, he'd been the most wanted spy in all of Scotland and one of the Royalist Resistance's most valuable resources. Second was Blair Macnab, who was like a sister to her friend Kirstie in the Cameron clan.

The next face that came into focus would have caused her to stumble had she been walking. It was Robbie.

He was now a Cameron, but she knew his true identity— he was the secret son of King Charles and the prince heir's younger twin brother. Very few knew of his existence, even fewer knew where he was hiding.

Which angered her, because of all the places in Scotland he should avoid, Edinburgh and anywhere near Parliament was on the top of the list. Alex had sent her to guard him on a couple of occasions before the Camerons had taken him in, and the young man had never been so careless before.

Brodie, Blair, and Robbie all knew she was the female face of the Royalist Resistance and she trusted them.

They dismounted and passed their horses off to the stable hands and walked up to the group who were standing alone, at a good distance from anyone who might hear. She stomped up and hissed to the lad, "What the hell are ye doing here?"

Brodie stepped in between Robbie and her. "I could ask ye the same thing, Isobel. Although I almost didnae recognize ye."

Grant took her hand and drew her to his side. "Dinnae talk to my wife that way if ye dinnae wish to leave my cousin a widow."

She couldn't help it. She started laughing. Grant hadn't told her who his cousin had married, but Brodie Cameron was the last man she'd expected to settle down. "Ye are married to Skye?" She'd never met the lass whose horse she'd been borrowing or whose old furniture now resided in the bedchamber she shared with her husband.

"And ye ken my wife?" Grant sounded jealous, and she rather liked that he might be.

"Aye." She nodded to her husband then glanced to the one man in the group she didn't know. She asked Brodie, "Can he be trusted?"

"Oh, aye. This is Finlay Cameron. We are escorting him and his wife home from visiting the king in England. If the king trusts him, ye can, too. And this is his wife, Blair Cameron."

"It's good to see ye are well, Blair. And 'tis nice to meet ye, Finlay. I have heard of yer connection to the king."

Blair threw her arms around Isobel. "I'm so happy yer safe. Ye saved many lives when ye told Kirstie about the plot to take out the Royalist lairds."

Isobel hugged her then, pleased she'd been of some help. When the lass drew back, Isobel turned and smiled up at her husband who seemed shocked that she knew most of the group and they knew of her secret. She glanced back to the retired spy. "My husband can be trusted as well."

"We're on our way home to Kentillie, but stopped over last night. We heard about the meeting today and thought we would lend our support and get word back to our laird on what is decided."

She took Grant's hand and whispered, "Brodie used to occasionally help the Resistance."

Then Brodie met Grant's glare. "I gave it up so that I could be a good husband to yer cousin. I can assure ye she is safe with me."

She turned to quiz Robbie. "And why are ye here? 'Tis no' safe and ye ken it."

"I had a chance to see my mother. I took it. And I was safe with the Camerons. They kept watch over me the whole time."

"Are ye planning to stay in the Highlands then?"

"Aye, my home is now with Clan Cameron and I dinnae plan on leaving again."

She was pleased Robbie had chosen to live among the Camerons because they were unwaveringly loyal to the king. His secret was too deadly to reveal to Grant among the mixed company. What if not all present were aware of the truth? She would wait until they were alone tonight and whisper to him that they had been in the presence of royalty.

• • •

"So, ye all ken who Isobel is?" Grant asked, feeling lost in the crowd. His wife had actually made friends despite her desire to push everyone away. He wondered if she realized she'd let these people into her life.

"Aye," Blair said. "She's helped a great many people."

His wife blushed. She was lovely, even with the slight bruise marring her cheek. By all appearance she was a lady and not a woman who would don men's clothes and run into battle. It gave him an idea.

He leaned in. "Ye can help keep her safe."

"Whatever we need to do." Blair nodded.

"We need witnesses. People who can verify she was nowhere near any of the Resistance skirmishes."

"That's a great plan. She can say she was with Skye when the battle that took yer brother-in-law happened. My wife would be happy to help." Brodie smiled.

He could count on Skye, his cousin, to vouch for Isobel should the need arise. A huge weight lifted from his chest.

"And she was with Kirstie and me on Macnab land the time before that," the petite blonde who'd embraced his wife added.

Even Finlay broke in. "And before that, she was visiting the Cameron laird's new wife at Kentillie."

As they stood there and continued to talk, a solid plan developed to defend his wife should the need arise.

Bells trilled through the yard, indicating it was time for them to file into the abbey and discuss how the Royalist clans could keep their religion without drawing the notice of those supporting Parliament. There was nothing they could do to stop the decree that only one religion should be practiced in Scotland, but they could keep their people safe.

While he'd not been able to stop Parliament from committing to the Covenants, today he had been able to assure his wife's safety.

Now there was only one threat left. Torsten Campbell. And he had to find the man soon, because losing Isobel would destroy him.

Chapter Nineteen

Although Isobel's husband and the other clan representatives hadn't been able to sway Parliament, the trip to Edinburgh had been a success. Grant had let her sit in on the meeting where the representatives of the Royalist clans talked about how to keep peace in the Highlands without drawing notice to their clans because they would continue to practice their religion in secret.

Friends she didn't know she had were also willing to stand up for her if Argyll ever learned of her involvement with the Resistance. And the best thing yet, as Grant's wife, she could advocate for the safety of the clans as well. She felt as if she had a whole new group of people to safeguard, her new family.

Shortly after the meeting, they retrieved the rest of their band and headed back to the Isle of Skye.

Isobel had become accustomed to the silent, steady pace they'd set; even the weather cooperated, providing sunny days with a pleasant wind. As the terrain turned more mountainous, she found peace in studying the patches of lavender on the inclines and security in the tree-lined paths.

After hours of scouring the landscapes, she felt certain Torsten Campbell was not lying in wait, but must be actively hunting for her. If he knew her whereabouts, there would have been a confrontation by now. They'd passed several groups of people on the roads north, farmers on their way to markets, mothers heading into the villages for supplies, and once some young children running with a black, wiry-haired dog whose protruding tongue was almost as long as its snout.

In the middle of their fourth day, the sun disappeared, clouds filled the sky, and a strong wind blew in a storm that pelted them so hard, it felt like tiny stinging daggers on her skin.

"We'll stop at the next village," her husband called from behind.

She recognized the little town and the church that stood in its center. Many priests in the area were connected with the Royalist Resistance, not as actual members, but as conduits between groups, delivering messages and storing knowledge. This village was near the middle of the Highlands and was the hub of Resistance activities.

"Isobel," Grant's voice broke in. She hadn't realized she'd stopped and was staring at the church. In the back of her mind, a plan had started to develop. "Did ye see something?" He seemed on edge for the first time in days.

"Nae. I've been here before." She couldn't lie to him. Aye, she'd seen this place before, but his tone had made it seem as if he were asking if she'd seen something threatening.

After stabling the horses and taking shelter in the only inn, the group gathered together at a large table in the common area. Despite the time of year, the storm had brought with it a drop in temperature, and the innkeepers lit a fire to keep the room warm.

Thunder boomed, shaking the windows. Grant scanned

the room, taking in every corner, every space, as if on the hunt for a lost item. When his gaze finally fell on her, he seemed to calm, taking a breath and leaning back as a maid brought a tray of ale.

She was quite uncomfortable, however—her exposed back to the open room and door to the outside sent shivers down her spine. She'd have to trust in the men with her that they would be vigilant. It felt odd putting her safety in others' hands, a little freeing and a lot terrifying.

Taking a sip of the warm amber liquid, she relaxed into the chair and studied the wall behind her husband. For her plan, she had to come up with an excuse to get over to that church.

Would he let her go? And would he follow?

Confession.

He couldn't follow her there, giving her just enough time alone with the priest.

"How's yer head today?" Annis, who was seated next to her, peered across the table to Ian.

"'Tis much better. The stabbing pain in it has finally gone away."

Taking another sip of ale, she noticed her hands had started to heal, although the ache in her side still bothered her when she mounted the horse or made awkward movements. And the bruise on her face had been barely noticeable this morning when she'd looked in the mirror.

"I still dinnae ken how ye took all three of them, lass." Ian shook his head.

"I've never seen a lass, much less a man, take on so many at one time." Owen, who was by Grant's side, gave her an appreciative nod, raising his glass to salute her.

"'Twas only because there was nae choice. And because they didnae think I was a threat until 'twas too late and Annis distracted them."

Looking down, she wasn't sure if she felt embarrassed, proud, or pleased with what she'd accomplished. The conflicting emotions gave her the excuse she needed.

"Grant, I noticed a church no' too far away. My conscience would feel better if I could go to confession."

He studied her with hardened suspicion, and her shoulders drooped, but then his gaze softened, as if he worried he'd hurt her feelings. "After we eat, I'll take ye over."

"Thank ye." She had the oddest urge to lean over the table and plant a kiss on his lips. Although they'd barely spoken the last few days, she enjoyed the sight of him laughing with his friends or his dark hair blowing back from his face as they trotted onward and he watched the shadows around them.

The fact he trusted her endeared him to her. To tell the truth, she'd found herself growing fond of him for some time. She'd never thought she would enjoy married life, but now that she was a wife, she could think of no better husband than the man who sat across from her. He might have been reading her thoughts, because his mouth twisted up in a wry grin.

After a meal of roasted meat with vegetables and stewed apples, Grant stepped across to where she was seated and took her hand, lacing his fingers between hers, an intimate touch they'd only shared at night. "The rain has lessened. I'll take ye now."

"Aye. I remember now, ye dinnae like the rain." She, on the other hand, loved the feel of the drops cleansing away false security that came with the beautiful weather.

They took off, running through the rain, fingers still entwined. It didn't take them long to reach the small church, but they were soaked. Stopping in the doorway, Grant's gaze slipped to the rise and fall of her chest then back up to her mouth. Under his scrutiny, her core heated and her mouth parted mere seconds before his lips brushed hers.

His warmth mingling with the cool droplets of rain sliding

off his dark hair onto her neck made her feel alive, made her feel wanted, told her that she was a woman to be desired.

He deepened the connection. As his tongue swept over hers, the doubts of the last few days faded. In the embrace she felt more than wanted, she felt cherished. She was lost in that kiss, lost to her husband, and…

A throat clearing caught her attention and Grant pulled back. Not only had she forgotten herself and possible dangers, but their surroundings. They were at the entrance to God's house.

Knowing the man would recognize her and welcome her, she asked, "Father, will ye hear my confession?"

"Aye, 'tis good to see ye, Isobel. And looks to be I should be listening to the sins of this one as well." She cringed when the priest acknowledged he knew her. She felt a pang of regret for not telling Grant about her ties to the church and the network of intelligence gathering that happened through these men of God. But the priests trusted her and she couldn't betray that faith.

Grant stiffened. "I'm her husband." His deep burr rolled over her in possessive waves, and there was a new edge to it— he was probably wondering how the priest knew her name.

The priest ushered them in and shut the door. "All right then, lass. This way." The man motioned Grant to a bench. "Ye can wait here."

Grant took a seat and his gaze pinned her with accusation. She had no doubt he'd be questioning her as soon as they were out of earshot of the holy man. Gulping, she wished the sweet man hadn't acknowledged their past acquaintance. It was going to be hard to explain away.

Shielding her embarrassment from Grant, she swirled to follow the priest.

"Married now are ye, lass?"

"Aye." She couldn't help but peek over her shoulder as

they made their way to the large wooden enclosure toward the side of the building. Grant was on the edge of the seat and listening intently, pinning her with an angry gaze that spoke of heated words to come.

"'Tis glad I am to see ye have found a man." Father John rubbed at his head, just where the balding patch on top hit his graying hair.

She started to confess she hadn't wanted this union, but she could no longer say it in truth—she'd come to care for her husband a great deal. But that was the problem. He mattered now, and people close to her always got hurt.

"I hope ye are truly here to confess. A wedded woman shouldnae be roaming the countryside with a group of renegades." His eyebrows, also flecked with silver, rose in question while he held a red curtain back from a booth.

"I just have one more thing to do and I can leave that all behind, but I need yer help." She entered once he drew the curtain, darkness enveloping her. She knelt, the cool dampness of the day and the old building invading her bones.

"Why are ye here today?" he asked after the curtain swung closed behind him. She peeked through hers to make sure Grant had not followed, but he still sat on the bench, glaring.

"Information." She leaned in, whispering into the screen.

"Aye." The skepticism in his voice signaled he didn't believe she would leave the Resistance.

"Torsten Campbell kens who I am. If he comes for me, I'm afraid he will hurt someone in my new clan." Saying the words sent renewed dread twisting through her.

"And have ye talked to yer husband or Alex about this?" The reproach in his voice was gentle but stern.

"Aye, but 'tis my place to protect them. 'Tis my fault I was recognized."

She was met with silence.

"Please, Father. I cannae let Torsten hurt anyone because of me."

"I do ken something. I ken he's been looking for ye, and he was just on MacLean lands. Probably figured ye were headed home."

Relief washed over her when she realized he hadn't gone to Argyll, or there would have been a whole army out looking for her. It just cemented what she believed—Torsten wanted the recognition for turning her over. His cousin's praise and admiration meant more to him than anything else.

"He probably kens ye are wed by now and will come looking for ye."

It was important she be vigilant the rest of the journey back.

"Isobel, ye have a way out. Tell yer husband and be done with this life. Ye deserve to be happy." She'd seen the priest on many occasions, but never told him of what had happened to her. She also knew her brother had been to this church as well and she wondered for the first time how Ross had felt about that day. He'd changed too. Did he place the blame at his own feet and had he confided in Father John?

"I will when the threat is gone. He may hurt someone if I dinnae go with him, and if I go he will take me to the earl."

The priest's sharp intake of breath let her know he understood the consequences of turning herself over.

"'Tis time ye started taking care of yerself instead of everyone else."

"I plan to be a good wife."

"And soon ye'll be a mother."

Tingles started in her shoulders and seeped down her back to land in her gut. She'd never considered being with child. How could she fight and put that life at risk? And when she had babes, she would have to stay near them and keep them safe.

How would she keep a wee bairn safe?

Suddenly, the space was too confining, closing in on her, and her breath came in short gasps.

His next words barely registered. "Do ye have anything ye wish to confess while we are here?"

"Aye." She held her trembling palms up. "I killed three men recently."

"Go on." She heard disappointment.

"If I hadnae, they would have killed my maid and one of the Cameron men."

"I see." And the resignation in his voice told her that Ross had indeed told the man of the past.

Despite what her husband and the rest of the Highlands believed, she had killed very few men and each time it had torn at her soul. It never brought her pleasure, only drenched her in sadness that men so cruel had to be dealt with in such a way.

"Will ye pray for me?" she choked out.

"Aye, ye ken I will. Now, get back to yer husband, tell him the truth, and leave all this behind. Ye are too good to live life as an outlaw."

• • •

Isobel's skin had paled in the time she'd been in the confessional with the short, balding priest. Grant was convinced the holy man had something to do with Alex Gordon's Resistance movement. The man had amassed an amazing network of spies and informants. And now, Grant was coming to learn too much about the group that sought to fight this war with violence instead of peace.

As his wife returned to him, the short man hurried up behind. "Was there anything ye would like to be confessing today?"

"Nae." Grabbing Isobel's hand, he dragged her toward the door. He wasn't going to accuse her of lying in God's house, so the sooner they got to their room at the inn the better.

As he stormed out into the early evening rain, his temper rose. Lightning flashed. He saw his uncle's face. Thunder crashed.

He was taken back to the day in the clearing. Isobel's bonny gaze met his and for a moment, they'd both been mesmerized. Until Torsten came upon her. Before he could get to her side, the man's sword slid across her arm. Then, he turned and saw his friend slashed by one of the men who had attacked their group. His assemblage of men, who had been on their way to Edinburgh to meet with Covenanters and Royalists and agree to a peaceful solution.

If he'd not been enthralled by Isobel, he'd have been by his friend's side. His friend might still be alive. But he'd seen Isobel and had been captivated, so much so, that he'd worked his way toward her to keep her safe from the large man hovering over her with a sword.

It dawned on him it hadn't been Isobel's fault, it had been his, for being distracted by her. *Damn*, he was still distracted by her every day. And here they were out in the open, men hunting her, and until they'd walked into that church he'd only been thinking of bedding her, not the danger she was in.

He had to get them back to Skye with haste. If he didn't get her back to safety, he could lose her, too. The faces of people flashed in his head—his uncle, his first wife, Lyall's brother, then Isobel. He could not lose Isobel.

"Slow down." She struggled with holding her skirts.

"I told ye. Nae more to do with that group."

"He isnae one of them."

"I amnae a fool."

"He just shares information," she pleaded.

"Which makes being around him dangerous."

"He is safe."

"Aye, he may be, but if others ken who he is, someone else may recognize ye. What if someone is watching him? Now they'll ken ye are here."

They reached the inn, and he flung open the door. Not letting Isobel go, he made directly for the stairs. It had been unwise to dine out in the open as well. What if someone had seen her? What if Torsten Campbell was around?

"'Twas a quick confession, Isobel. I dinnae think ye covered everything." Boyd chortled from the room, but Grant already had her halfway up the steps.

Once they were in the room, he bolted the door. "Why were we there?"

"To confess." She tilted her chin up at him.

"Nae. What did ye ask him?"

"If he had heard where Torsten Campbell was."

"I told ye to let me handle that."

"Well ye've done a fine job of ignoring it from what I can see. Yer no' handling a thing. Nothing except yer silly quest for peace."

His fists clenched. Is that what she thought? That he'd neglected protecting her? He'd considered telling her his plan, but if he did, she might try to stop him, or worse, attempt to be present for the confrontation. She was capable of defending herself, but last time she'd faced Torsten, she'd almost died, and he couldn't keep his wits if he thought her in danger.

And did she think his desire to find a solution to the Highlands problems made him foolish?

She looked at him with soulful brown eyes, remorseful and pleading. She twined her fingers with his, lessening the tension. "I am sorry. 'Tis no' a small thing to wish peace. I wish it, too, and I admire that ye so openly argue for it. I hope one day I have the faith ye do in humanity."

She respected him? He'd not seen past her arguing and mistrustful ways, but the sincerity in her gaze and the honesty in her voice gave him hope they could share more in common than he'd thought possible.

"Please forgive me for rushing to see the bad instead of the good." She placed a hand on his chest.

He nodded, pulled her in, and relaxed at the feel of her in his arms.

"I never told ye why I was at that battle," she whispered as she nestled into him. "Those men were going to kill the Cameron brothers because of their religion, no' because of anything they had done. I kenned 'twould destroy Kirstie if something had happened to them."

He knew the Cameron laird and his younger brother had gone to Edinburgh for a meeting that ended with an attack on Royalist lairds. There were other parties attacked on the journey as well, and those groups had not fared as well as his, losing many lives.

He'd never made it to Edinburgh because of his friend's death, and he had to concede that if the Royalist Resistance had not been waiting to help his men, everyone in his party, including him, could be dead.

"I only wanted a peace of sorts. I just wanted my friend's family safe and I had to watch over Stew. He was too young to be out there. Someone had to protect him." Isobel continued as his thoughts simmered, "I just want to keep ye safe."

The admission stung, because he wasn't sure if she had become as attached to him as he was to her. At the same time, it freed the part of him he'd been holding back. "I ken now, 'twas no' ye I was angry with all this time. 'Twas me for letting my guard down in yer presence the first time I saw ye. If I let that happen again, I'm afraid I could lose ye."

As the rain pounded on the window, he tightened his

grip, drawing her near. He remembered another day where the rain beat down relentlessly, a battle between two men. It was the afternoon that had colored every moment of his life since. A vision of his uncle's head falling from strong shoulders after the disagreement with the MacLeods.

He would not let that happen to his wife. If Torsten Campbell wouldn't accept his offer, there would be war because he refused to hand the lass in his arms over to the Earl of Argyll.

Chapter Twenty

Isobel studied the shadows on the ceiling as she lay in bed alone. She usually treasured her time of solitude, but now she'd grown accustomed to falling asleep with her husband next to her. It had become so easy to be with him and the rest of their group and she found, for the first time in years, she longed for their company instead of shunning relationships. The new sense of belonging frightened her.

She and Grant had dined in their room tonight, she assumed because he was worried about her being seen, which she had to admit was a valid concern now that she was certain Torsten was looking for her. She wished she could go back and ask the priest if there had been others with him. She needed to know if he'd told anyone, although she doubted it, if someone else took her to Argyll, he wouldn't get the credit and she knew the Covenanters he associated with were not honorable men.

Grant had taken her to bed, the pace slow and gentle, but somehow even more intense than their previous bed play. Something had shifted between them and although she wanted to give in to the emotions and throw herself into being a perfect wife for him, she couldn't afford to until she'd solved the problem of Torsten Campbell.

If Torsten was looking for her on MacLean lands, she needed to get there to find him before he came across someone she cared about. She'd consider trying to get a message to one of her brothers, but Grant had made it clear any further contact with someone who dealt with the Resistance wouldn't be tolerated. He wouldn't even let her go back to the priest to have him deliver her message through the communication chain. Writing and sending a letter through the post was the fastest way to let the news fall into someone else's hands and then everyone would know who she was, so that option was not viable, either.

Her best recourse would be to talk to Grant about visiting her family when they returned to Skye. It would be a legitimate trip because there were a few things from home she'd like to bring with her and her family had dropped her on Grant's island with barely anything that was her own. He would have to let her collect her belongings.

Grant would probably send for her items if she wished, but how was she to protect him and Annis if she couldn't take care of the threat? Once Torsten Campbell was gone, she'd devote herself to her husband and new family and she would find a way to fit in.

At peace with her decision, she finally closed her eyes and hoped she would rest.

The most vivid dream of that day on the road to Edinburgh invaded her sleep. It was the day she'd first seen Grant. This time, the battle went well and all the Covenanters were defeated. She saw Grant from a distance, but he didn't see her and he turned with his friend, mounted his horse and rode away without ever meeting her eyes. She called out to him, but he never turned back.

She woke as Grant's arm wrapped around her, but the dream had left her hollow. She burrowed into his arms, looking for the security they offered and the assurance that he wouldn't leave her. She barely slept the remainder of the evening.

• • •

The next day was clear and they left just as the rooster called the last of its crowing. They rode hard all day, only stopping for short meals. That night, intense dreams invaded her sleep, leaving her restless and apprehensive. The one that lingered in her thoughts the following day, making her stomach turn, was the dream about the kitten she'd found on the side of the road. This time when opening the sack, she found a baby, but instead of telling her she should take care of it as he had the furry creature, Grant took the babe and left her on the side of the embankment, telling her she'd never be able to protect something so precious.

The next several days passed in the same haze as the scenery changed, the mountains becoming higher, the passes more treacherous, and the lavender on the sides of the hills blurring by. Even the air felt cleaner as they moved farther away from the city and the sites of battles she'd witnessed.

Before she knew it, the sun was setting on another day and they were at the shore waiting for a boat to ferry them across to Cairntay, the MacDonald stronghold that sat high on the cliffs on the other side. Grant's shoulders relaxed for the first time in days. It gave her a sense of pride in this place to see her husband affected by just the proximity to his home. She was pleased he looked more at ease, but it was almost time to put her plan into motion.

As the boat slid into the shoreline, Grant took her hand. "Let's go home." It sounded like he wanted her there, too, and she should be a part of it.

"Aye." She smiled at him as he led her toward the vessel, and she wanted that dream again, the one she'd held as a child, where she had a husband who loved her and a family and didn't have to think about safety.

A large black shadow cooled her skin as it slid over her body. A black bird headed in the direction they'd just come from, reminding her she wasn't safe. And because of her, her husband and their clan weren't safe, either.

Boyd escorted the still limping Annis and got her to a railing she could hold on to. Strolling up beside her maid as the boat started its journey across the water, Isobel asked, "Are ye looking forward to seeing yer baker?"

"Aye, I am. I have missed him terribly."

The waters were moving swiftly, guiding the boat out to sea as the men fought against the current, rowing massive oars, shuttling them toward the green hills and rocky cliffs on the opposite site.

"Ye deserve a few days' rest. Stay off yer feet and ye can come back next week when ye've had time to mend."

"Nae, I'll be fine."

"Ye need to let it heal." And she needed to sneak away. She couldn't have Annis following her if Grant let her visit her brothers, especially because she might find Torsten Campbell there. Her maid needed to stay on Skye where she was safe.

"Very well, as long as ye promise me ye will get some sleep. Ye look exhausted."

"I havenae been sleeping. I'm having dreams so real I can feel them, and they willnae let me rest."

Annis smiled as if she'd just told the lass her biggest secret.

"What?"

"Ye are with child." The lass clasped her hands together.

"Nae." She wasn't ready for that. "Why would ye think something so silly?"

"When was the last time ye had yer courses?"

Her fingers curled around the railing as the world tilted. She'd not even noticed, being so distracted by her new environment and then the journey to Edinburgh and the threat of Torsten. How had she missed the signs?

Her mouth fell open, but no sound came out as it dawned on her that she'd not bled since before her wedding to Grant. She swallowed mixed emotions—fear and delight mingled in equal measure—and her arms prickled as the mist from the water tickled her skin.

"My older sister calls them mother's visions. She was plagued with them for both of her pregnancies."

Why had she not known these things? What was she going to do?

A bairn.

Her hand drifted to her belly as she thought about the tiny life hidden within, someone to protect and guard. A little life who needed to stay close to Cairntay for safety, who would need its mother nearby.

Who would need her.

Och, how would she tell Grant?

He'd never let her leave for MacLean lands if he knew she was with child. Her other hand came to cover her mouth, then she let it fall back to her side. "But I havenae been sick. I thought mothers were always ill."

"Nae, only some. I'm certain ye are. I've seen it enough with my large family." Annis laughed.

She attempted to control the trembling in her fingers. If she'd not shut her mother out all those years ago, maybe she would have known these things. "Ye cannae tell anyone." Annis looked confused. "Just let me accept it before we say anything."

The lass nodded.

A hand touched the small of her back and she jumped.

"Och, settle down there. We are almost safe and home." Grant moved to stand beside her.

Her husband's gaze drifted back to the shoreline, his ruggedly handsome features appraising his home as if it was the most beautiful place he'd ever seen, as if he was happy to come back. She had to admit it looked magical and impregnable in the fading light—a combination of the charmed home the child in her had wanted and the fortress the grown woman in her needed.

She'd never felt that way on MacLean lands. Perhaps it was because she'd never felt safe after the attack.

Her own gaze drifted in that direction, and she wondered if she would ever feel as he did. Could this place truly give her the security she'd missed all these years? Tears stung at the innocence she had lost. She would never let that happen to her child.

Would her babe be protected by the Isle of Skye's cliffs and the strong gray stone of the castle on the hill? Cairntay appeared to be an impenetrable stronghold, and the men told stories of failed invasion attempts where its imposing walls had protected Clan MacDonald.

Once Torsten Campbell was gone, she thought so.

Regret took hold because it was her that had put them all in jeopardy, the very thing she'd been trying to avoid. If Argyll discovered who she was, he would come after the MacDonald clan for protecting her. She had put Grant, Annis, and now her babe at risk. She had her own people to protect now and she couldn't do that and be associated with the notorious group.

This was her fresh start. This place and this man and his child could fill the void and give her the peace she'd once craved.

Later, after bathing, having a large meal, and being reunited with the little furry creature, she fought to hold her eyes open. She waited for Grant to return, but he didn't.

· · ·

"I need men hidden on the other shore." Grant leaned back in the chair in his father's study. He arched his shoulders back and stretched his head to one side then the other, but it did little to assuage his tight muscles.

He'd thought once they were home the tension would lessen, but the threat to Isobel felt intensified. At least when they'd been moving about, she would have been harder to track, but now that they were back on MacDonald lands, she was well protected, but also easy to find. He'd have to post guards on her and make sure she didn't leave the castle until he'd eliminated the danger.

"Why?" The lack of worry in Alastair MacDonald's tone denoted the trust of a man who believed in him unconditionally. His father was a tough man, and he had earned Grant's respect over the years. The laird moved to a table on the side of the room, picked up a decanter, and poured them both a dram of whisky.

"Torsten Campbell will be coming for Isobel." The pressure on his chest at just saying the words threatened to steal his breath. "He's been looking for her on MacLean lands, and I sent word that I wanted his audience."

The laird nodded, his lips quirking to one side as they often did when he was deep in thought.

"He'll be here. And nae, it seems he wants the reward for finding her and willnae risk telling anyone else."

"I believe ye are correct if he has no' betrayed her so far." His father paced as he did when he was mulling over a problem.

"I'm going to offer him Lyall's dowry." He'd been thinking on the matter since the day he'd sent the missive to the Campbell for a meeting. Neither he nor the clan needed it, and it felt right. Despite their short time together, he knew Lyall would want him to be happy.

His father coughed, choking on the whisky he'd just sipped. "But 'tis a fortune."

"Lyall was a generous woman. She would have wanted it. I think she would have liked Isobel."

"Ye have had a change of heart."

He gave a slight nod as he assessed all the things he'd learned about Isobel on their journey, and how he wanted nothing more for her than to have a life free of worry, to be able to form relationships again, and to feel safe.

"She isnae who I thought she was. But there's more to my plan. I think 'tis necessary Torsten stay on Skye with us. He could live prosperously and never have to want for anything, but I dinnae trust him to take the money and still keep his mouth shut."

"I agree."

"Ye will honor the deal and put him under MacDonald protection?"

"Aye. Ye have my blessing." Somewhere in his father's deep burr and firm words, he heard approval, maybe even pride.

It was the right thing. If the MacLeans had offered a dowry for Isobel, he'd have thrown that in as well.

"Why do ye need men?" The laird settled into the chair behind his desk.

"The Campbell man may not accept the coin and our hospitality. I cannae take the risk no harm will come to Isobel or that he'll not come back with an army and attack the clan. If a deal is not reached, I'll have to kill him."

"I am proud of ye, son."

A moment of silence passed as his father's gaze drifted to the portrait that hung to the left of the fireplace. A young man stared back at them with similar features to his father's, a reckless spirit shining in his eyes.

"My brother would be, too." A sheen glistened on his father's eyes.

The laird stood and returned to the tray on the table, pouring a healthy serving of whisky into two more glasses. Striding back toward him, his father took Grant's empty cup and offered the full one. He accepted it. "I didnae tell ye everything that happened that day. I couldn't find the words and then there was never a good time because each time yer uncle's name was mentioned ye closed yerself off so I just couldnae do it." His father took a big gulp, seeming to be immune to the potent liquid, but then his eyes clouded.

"The MacLeods werenae offering him an agreement. It was all for show. Glen let his guard down and that's when he was stabbed. What ye saw that day, when it looked like he had attacked first, it wasnae true. When Glen drew his sword, he was already wounded and defending himself."

Chills erupted on his shoulders and spread to his arms and back. Implications washed over him as everything he'd believed came crashing down around him. His uncle had gone out with peace in mind and had never made it home.

Grant spent the next several hours planning with his father.

Later, as Grant entered his chamber to find his wife asleep, the kitten curled up near her feet, he studied Isobel in the candlelight. He had a sinking feeling, especially after the talk with his father, Torsten wouldn't accept the bargain. The only way to truly protect his wife might be to take out the man who would see her harmed.

Not wanting to wake her, he undressed, blew out the candle, and slid under the blankets to join her. The last time they had shared this bed, he barely knew her. Now, he felt as if his universe revolved around the little lass and he drew her near, knowing he would do whatever it took to keep her safe and confident he had the MacDonald clan behind him.

The next morning when he woke, he found his wife petting the creature as it sat on her chest. A light rumbling sound vibrated from the happy cat. "I think he missed ye."

Isobel turned toward him and continued to massage its ears, cheek and neck. "It's a she."

"How do ye ken?" Resting on one elbow, he scratched the scruffy thing's neck. It leaned into his touch.

"The person who watched her while we were gone told me. She also said it kept coming up here looking for me and crying." Her sideways smirk held a suggestion of a smile, like she was pleased the little fluffy creature had chosen her.

"Well, whether or no' ye want the thing, it wants ye." It was kind of like him. He wanted her, but he'd never stopped to think how she felt. She seemed more comfortable with him, but would she be happy here with the MacDonalds, with him, without the Resistance?

"Daracha," Isobel said as her gaze drifted from him down to the creature. Now the smile was genuine.

"What?"

"That's her name. We can't keep calling her 'it'."

Awareness struck him. She had decided to make this marriage work. If she hadn't formed an attachment to him, she had at least bonded with the cat, something he guessed she'd not done since her childhood. And Isobel had said "we." A pressure on his chest lifted, because she had decided she belonged here, with him.

"So ye've decided, ye like it here and ye'll stay." He tensed with need for her, to claim her once again and seal their life together.

"Aye."

He scooped up the kitten, put it on the other side of him, then leaned in to give his wife a kiss. His lips collided with hers, pure joy spreading through him as she leaned into his embrace.

A knock sounded and he reluctantly pulled back. "Och, 'tis too early for Annis."

"Nae, I sent her home for a few days. She shouldnae be here."

The noise sounded again, this time a deeper, more urgent pounding.

"Yes?" he called out.

"Grant," Boyd said.

"What?"

"Ye are needed below."

Resignation washed over him as a dark foreboding shadowed the joy he'd felt only moments earlier. He and his father had agreed to call a council this morning to discuss the danger facing the clan, but the sun wasn't even up.

"Looks like we'll have to do this later."

Isobel nodded as he slid from the covers.

The cat, who had jumped to the floor, paced around him, crying as if hurt. "What's wrong, wee one?" It rubbed against his calf then started to the door before looking back and meowing at him again.

"She's probably hungry and needs to go out."

After dressing quickly, he opened the door to let Daracha out, then turned back to look at the sleepy lass he was leaving.

A moment of panic assailed him at the thought of her wandering around on her own—she seemed to find trouble anytime he left her to her own devices, and he'd not had a chance to talk to her yet about the threat headed their way. "Stay in the castle until I can talk to ye. I'll be back as soon as I can."

She stretched and nodded.

Satisfied she might just go back to sleep, he stepped through the door, shut it, and met Boyd in the hall.

Daracha bounded for the stairs and then pounced out of sight.

Boyd started, "He's on the other shore on the land of Clan Ranald."

That was where they had been just yesterday before crossing over to Skye. "Do ye ken if he brought men with him?"

They reached the bottom of the stairs and rounded the corner toward his father's study. "I dinnae ken yet. The laird just sent me to fetch ye."

Grant pushed in the door and was not only met by his father but a roomful of men with silent, stony faces. Boyd followed and clicked the door shut behind them.

"What has happened?"

His father pulled out a piece of parchment, leaned forward on his elbows, and began reading.

MacDonald,

I'm here for the rebel. She needs to face justice for her crimes. I'll be waiting at the Black Grouse tavern at sunset tonight. I have men watching both yer shoreline and the tavern, so only send the lass. If more come, I'll be forced to tell Argyll ye are harboring a fugitive. And ye ken what he's done to MacDonalds in the past. Dinnae give him a reason to bring war to yer clan over a worthless criminal.

A concerned Campbell

His father dropped the missive on his desk and peered across the room at him. Surely, his father wouldn't expect him to hand her over. But the thought of all the innocent

MacDonalds murdered on Rathlin Island on Ireland's shores by Argyll's men because they were kin made his pulse hammer out a furious pace that turned his stomach.

"What do ye wish to do, Grant?"

It was the moment he'd always dreaded, when his father had him make decisions for the clan. Was it a test, or would his father go with his wishes? Either way, the clan had to come first, but he would find a way to keep Isobel safe no matter the cost to him.

"She is a MacDonald now. One of us. We willnae hand her over to a Campbell."

The laird nodded his approval, and relief flooded him that his father would stand beside them.

"We must contain this before he can get to Argyll, then. Let's come up with a better plan now that we ken where he is."

They spent the next few hours devising plans to keep his wife and the clan safe. When Grant finally emerged from the room, he headed straight toward their chamber to discover his wife missing.

Damn, he'd not even had the time to put guards on her. What if Torsten had come to the Isle of Skye for her?

He couldn't lose someone else. No, it was more than that. He couldn't lose Isobel. He had cared for his last wife as his friend, but it was more with her. Somehow she'd become part of who he was, of who he wanted to be. He could no longer see life without her.

A shiver ran down his spine and he rushed from the room to find her. Relief flooded him when he found her at a table with his mother, laughing as she rubbed the kitten that sat in her lap.

"Mother, can we have a few moments?"

Fenella MacDonald jumped up to rush over and draw him into a tight, reassuring embrace. He returned the hug.

"Aye. I'm so pleased ye two are back." Looking to Isobel, she pulled back and continued, "I'll be just outside. When ye are done come find me and I'll introduce ye to the cousins ye havenae yet met."

"Aye, I'd like that."

Grant studied his wife, pleased that she and his mother seemed to be forming a bond as well.

Although Isobel wore a dark blue gown that had been made for her and given to her last night upon their return, the ties were loose and while he could see she had tried to pin up her hair, strands fell around her face, giving her the appearance of a woman who had been thoroughly ravished. Suddenly, he wanted to scoop her up and rush to their chamber to do just that.

But there were more important things that had to be taken care of first.

Isobel said, "I'd like to go collect my belongings."

"What belongings?" He didn't think she'd forgotten anything on their trip.

"From my old home."

A chill ran down his backbone. How could she even think of leaving right now? "I'll send for them."

"Nae, I'd like to go see my brothers."

Something about her persistence clicked—she knew exactly what she was doing and he wasn't going to have it. Clenching his fists, he couldn't help the anger creeping into his tone. "Then I'll ask them to come for a visit."

"I'd like to go." She squared her shoulders, making it seem almost like an order.

Reserve gone, his temper sprang from the place he'd tried to keep hidden. "Until the threat is taken care of, ye will be going nowhere." His words echoed through the empty hall, reverberating almost like a physical blow. He softened his tone. "Ye are safer here."

"We cannae sit around and do nothing about it." Her gaze pinned him with accusation.

"That is exactly what ye'll do. I'll have Owen and Ian guard ye until 'tis sorted out."

"And we ken how well that worked out last time." She stood, attempting to get an even footing with him, but he still stood several inches taller than her. Isobel had proven she was capable of handling herself, but also that she was good at getting into trouble.

"Ye will stay here on Skye for now." He closed the distance between them and reached for her cheek, but she pulled back. "I promise I'll take ye soon."

Her sad gaze spoke of mistrust and stabbed at his heart. "Very well." Skirting around him, she made her way for the door, but it didn't seem right—she wouldn't give in that easily. He'd have to find his friends. They were the only ones he trusted to keep her safe from Torsten Campbell and from herself.

A storm had rolled in and the walls inside the castle grew colder as he made his way back to his father's study, hoping the men hadn't gone far. Owen was still talking amongst the MacDonalds. Thunder boomed and he felt a shift in the air. A damp cool breeze blew in through the window.

"I need ye and Boyd to keep watch on Isobel."

"Aye. Where is she?"

"With my mother. I think they were going to stay near the castle. Especially with the threat of the storm."

Owen started off in search of her, but only minutes later he rushed in. "Isobel is no' with yer mother. And she's no' in yer chamber."

Chapter Twenty-One

Fear and anger ripped at Grant's insides as he ran through the castle looking for Isobel. Surely she wouldn't have gone out looking for Torsten. He hadn't even had a chance to tell her how close the menace was.

He finally found a lad in the kitchen shooing Daracha from a chair as he mixed something in a bowl.

"Have ye seen my wife?"

"Aye, she went out that way just a few minutes ago." The lad pointed to the door with a long wooden spoon.

He rushed through the open door, cold wet droplets assailing him as he dashed toward the nearest people who had taken cover beneath the overhang of the healer's cottage roof.

Someone nodded that they'd seen her. His heart stopped beating when the man pointed to the beach—the same stretch of land Torsten Campbell was probably watching. He had to get to her before she exposed herself to the arse on the other side.

Running, he paid little heed to the rain pelting his eyes,

only brushed his hair back to see the stones that formed a path down the steep embankment to the shore below.

She'd only made it down a few steps when he reached her. He snaked his arm across her waist and pulled her back into his chest. She struggled and he realized she hadn't seen him coming. "'Tis me, wife."

Still, she tried to pull away but he couldn't let her go any farther. He spied a patch of bushes a few steps away and said a quick prayer they were enough to shield her from anyone watching. Loosening his grip, he freed her, took her hand, and urged her back upward, careful to watch over his shoulder at the other shore for movement.

Once they'd cleared the top, he inhaled. While towing her across the muddy yard, he felt her stumble. Guilt at his haste niggled him, but it didn't replace the relief he felt for getting to her in time or the fear he'd felt at the thought of Torsten Campbell delivering her to the Earl of Argyll.

As soon as they entered the castle and the rain was no longer beating down on them, his wife dug in her heels. "What are ye doing?"

He rounded on her, anger taking place of the fear. "What the hell do ye think ye were doing?"

She flinched, her eyes growing larger. Right now, he didn't mind her trepidation, in fact she needed a healthy dose if he was to keep her safe until this mess was over.

"Yer mother was called to the hall to have an audience with a woman from the village, so I was just going to go for a walk."

"In the rain?"

"Aye. It clears my head."

"I told ye no' to leave the castle."

"So now that we are home, I'm relegated to prisoner again?" She pushed past him, starting for the great hall.

"Halt!" He grabbed her hand and lugged her toward the

stairs. "We arenae done."

He trudged up the stairs and hauled her into their chamber, her skirts swirling as he twirled her into the space and slammed the door behind them.

She looked sad, disappointed. He could take her anger, but not this. He didn't like it.

"I just need time to think. 'Tis my fault he's out there."

"The clan and I have a plan, but if he finds ye first, it willnae work." He took her hand, his tone pinning her with conviction, hoping to show her he had the situation well in hand.

"I promise once 'tis dealt with, I'll no' go back to the Resistance." Her eyes pleaded and he moved closer, the exotic scent she wore washing over him, reassuring him that she was still here. "Does that mean that ye can be happy here?"

"Aye, it does. I will stay here to keep our clan safe, to keep watch over ye and Annis."

He took her fingers in his, and his heart burst with pride and joy.

"And ye have to see why I cannae stand back and let ye be hurt for my mistake. I have to be the one to do it." Her gaze hardened.

"Do ye think I would let ye risk confronting Torsten on yer own?

"I have to ken ye are safe and our babe will be safe."

Every muscle in his body went numb as everything in the room but Isobel blurred. "Isobel." Her name came out hoarse, like the time he'd lost it for several days.

She pulled free and moved as if she would head for the door.

"Look at me." He had a clear view of her face from the light trickling in from the window. "'Tis another reason ye cannae go down to that beach now."

He drew her in, holding her close as the smell that was his

wife, some kind of flower mixed with the fresh rain, assaulted his senses and threatened to drive him mad. He felt a strange urge to hold on, like his arms were the only thing keeping her moored to him, and she might sail away and never be seen again if he let go.

"I dinnae understand." Her soft voice was muffled by his shoulder as he nuzzled into her.

He didn't, either. He only knew that the whole world was right here in his arms. She was his everything and he didn't know how it had happened. Isobel MacLean MacDonald, wanted member of the Royalist Rebels, had become the most important person in his life. And now, they were going to bring a wee little bairn into the world.

"Ye cannae go down there because Torsten Campbell is just on the other side of the water."

She blinked then put her hands on his chest and pushed, but he didn't let go. "Why did ye nae tell me?"

"Because I didnae want ye doing something foolish like going down there to face him on yer own."

"And ye would let me believe ye knew nothing of his whereabouts?"

"Ye cannae go out there, because I cannae lose ye."

She stilled in his arms and he wondered if he'd revealed too much.

But once he started, he couldn't stop. "I've lost too many people I care about and if something happened to ye, I dinnae ken what I would do." His throat hurt as he choked out the words, afraid voicing them might make her vanish into a cloud of smoke or the mist that rolled out with the dawning of the sun.

He was kissing her cheeks, inhaling her fresh scent, and he knew he'd never look at the rain the same way. Storms were turbulent and dangerous, but were also fresh and cleared the mind, just like his Isobel.

His mouth fell to her ear and he whispered words he'd thought until now were a curse, the one thing he had to say before it burned a hole in his chest and consumed him. "I love ye."

When he pulled back, he thought he saw a mist in her eyes, but he wasn't certain. She didn't return his words, but she rose up on her toes, pulled him down, and pressed her lips to his.

If she didn't feel the same, it would crush him, but right now, he would revel in the knowledge that he'd been lucky enough to be forced to marry the one woman in all of Scotland who had been able to find her way into his heart.

. . .

Grant's words washed over her in waves. She'd thought she misunderstood, but as he stilled and waited for her to reply, they crashed into her senses.

He loved her.

How was that possible?

But his warm breath stole across her and shivers ran through her body, making her feel as if she were engulfed in a whirlwind of leaves that tickled her skin. He nibbled her ear and her hands clenched onto him for balance. He'd thrown everything she knew into imbalance and she was terrified, no, she was exhilarated.

She held on, trembling, needing balance, but also needing the clarity that only his touch gave. They were in their room, but she could have been anywhere. He did that to her, made her lose herself, but at the same time it was like she knew everything when she was in his arms.

Their positions shifted as he backed her toward their bed. And she went willingly, with glee.

She'd not known Torsten was near, but her husband was

right—had she been aware, she would have gone straight for him, sword drawn.

Her breath became shallow. She'd let this man before her find his way into a place in her heart she'd never given to anyone.

The realization left her feeling vulnerable and scared, weak and unsure, but his words made her heart beat faster. She'd done the one thing she'd promised herself she'd never let happen—she had let him in, wholly, completely. How had this happened?

Pushing away, she walked to the window to take in air that wouldn't ease the crushing pressure on her chest. The Resistance had been forgotten, and she'd become immersed in her new life with her husband. He had become her world.

Arms encircled her waist, drawing her into the solid frame of her husband. She breathed him in—the scent of rain and a male musk that was his alone—relishing the feel of being in Grant's arms. Still wrapped in his embrace, she turned, and her hands rose to his cheeks.

She loved him, too. Loved him so hard that it would destroy her if he walked away from her.

She felt the words, but she couldn't say them. It had been a shock to discover them written on her heart, so instead she said, "Kiss me, husband." A possessive, almost primitive joy washed over her as she acknowledged he belonged to her as much as she belonged to him.

Blue eyes dilated as desire blazed at her in his gaze. She licked her lips, letting them part as his mouth met hers. With the first stroke of his tongue, she teared at the emotions sweeping through her as, for the first time, she opened to him completely, finally allowing her heart to admit he owned her soul.

She could feel the raw need contained in his caress. How did she deserve such a boon? She would guard this man with everything she possessed. She would not lose him.

Her core tightened and moisture pooled at the juncture of her legs, waiting for the thick bulge that pressed into her hip. She shimmied back and forth, enjoying the pressure of his desire for her.

Groaning into her mouth, his kiss deepened as his grip around her middle tightened. Sparks ignited on her back as his fingers worked at the ribbons holding her gown to her heated skin. After fumbling for a few moments with no success, he drew back, his gaze pinning her with hunger. Her mouth curved up at the knowledge Grant MacDonald wanted her above all others.

"Turn around." His hoarse command signaled he was on the frenzied edge of needing to possess her. She did as he ordered, pulling her unbound hair over her shoulder to give him better access to the bindings of her gown.

As the garment loosened, he raised her arms and held them aloft while he pulled the material over her head. A tremble wracked her shoulders once he again engulfed her, his lips closing in on the part of her neck that sent tingles through her body and gooseflesh erupting on her skin. As he caressed her skin, she unfastened her skirt, her desire to be naked beneath him so intense that she couldn't wait. The material fell to the floor.

She kicked out of her slippers, relieved to be free of the wet shoes. Grant released her and unbelted his plaid, then tossed it onto the nearby chair. She bent to roll down her stockings, not removing her gaze from the sinewy form of her husband.

How lucky she had been when her family had forced her into this marriage. They could have easily foisted her off on someone less attractive or a man she didn't respect. Grant had proven he was a leader who would do what it took to keep his people happy and safe. And she saw now that his desire to seek the most peaceful resolution to a conflict made him noble and brave.

He bent to unlace his boots, rewarding her with a glimpse of the golden muscles that stretched across his broad shoulders. After kicking them to the side, he removed his stockings and straightened.

She took a step toward him.

Warm hands rested on her thighs, grasped the material of her shift and slowly drew it up to leave her bare before him, her body on display for his perusal. The garment slipped from his hand and he moved in to recapture her, his warm hard body melding with hers, his skin heating her flesh as her engorged nipples pushed into his chest, sending deafening waves of need crashing down on her, just as his mouth met hers.

There was only Grant and her. Everything else fell away.

He scooped her off her feet. His gaze never left hers, the fevered need she saw there enthralling and mesmerizing her. She leaned into him, enjoying the sensation of being cherished, like a treasure he coveted, like he would never mistake her for a boy. She felt like a woman.

After laying her down on the plush blankets, he climbed onto the bed, positioning himself between her legs and bracing his solid form above her. His sapphire gaze bared his soul—she could see the emotion in their mesmerizing depths. When the head of his erection penetrated her folds, she rose up to meet him, seeking out the connection, the completion of belonging to each other.

Her hands rose and pulled his hips closer and held on, grounding her as waves of bliss and complete abandonment took root. Grant moved in and out slowly at a measured pace, one that had her yearning for him to plunge harder but also feeling this deliberate torture was right and meant something more. Her eyes teared at the overwhelming connection that had formed between them.

Then she was gasping.

Tension built within her so quickly she called out, "Grant," in surprise. But then tremors took over as rational thought fled and she was locked in on him. Her soul mingled with his as she gave in and let the pleasure take over, drowning her in a tidal wave of sensation and ultimate trust. Just as she came to her senses, her husband stiffened above her, his rhythm faltering, and he spilled his seed inside her.

A few moments later, he slid from her, rolling onto his back. He drew her into the spot between his shoulder and chest, cradling her in his embrace. It seemed like only seconds before the rise and fall of his chest slowed. Sighing, she snuggled in closer and thought about his confession. She tried to whisper she loved him, too, but her mouth remained sealed tight. She felt the words, knew them to be true, but something held them back, as if the last part of her that didn't trust wouldn't let her.

Chapter Twenty-Two

Grant jerked awake and startled Isobel. "I have to go."

"Why the hurry? 'Tis storming something fierce out there." She didn't want him to leave. The thought of him out with Torsten tore at every fiber of her being.

After giving her a small kiss on the lips, he slid from beneath the covers and while she stayed beneath them, cold started to creep in.

"I have some things I need to see to. Dinnae leave the castle. I'll tell ye when 'tis safe to do so again."

Ah, he had most likely been in with the other men this morning devising their final strategy for facing Torsten.

"What is the plan? I can help." She sat up to watch him pull his shirt over his head, holding the blankets near her chest as it beat uncontrollably.

"Ye can help by staying safe." He didn't understand. Her heart might stop while he was out there without her. She had to be there to keep him safe.

"'Tis my fault he is here."

"I have a more than fair offer for him."

"He willnae accept."

Once he'd pulled his plaid on, Grant pinned it in place then reached for his stockings and boots. "I will do what must be done."

"Ye will let me come." She flung back the covers, jumped out of bed, and grabbed her shift, hastily donning it as she hopped toward him, pulling on her own stockings. He was already dressed and standing.

"If ye are there, I will be distracted. 'Tis what happened when Lyall's brother died. 'Twas my fault, because I was watching ye that day. And if something happened to ye because I was distracted, I would never forgive myself." His brows shot up and a sad sheen entered the depths of his eyes. "Ye will stay here and the matter will be dealt with by the morning." He drew her in and held her close. She was somewhere between the verge of tears and the tirade of a tantrum.

He headed for the door and paused. Without turning to look at her, he said, "I cannae watch ye die."

Then, peeking over his shoulder, added, "I have some business to see to. Will ye meet me for the midday meal?"

"I will." She relaxed as she realized he wasn't rushing out to face the threat now.

After pulling open the door, his gaze turned away as he stepped out into the hall and shut the door behind him.

Hours later, after they had taken a mostly silent meal together, he escorted her back up to their chamber. Once inside, he took her in a passionate embrace. The kiss was so intense, it left her feeling pliant as she molded into his body, searching for more.

Grant drew back, but still held her in his arms.

"Ye and our babe are the most important people in my life. If something happened to ye, it would destroy me. Ye will stay in this room until I return." It was an order, from her husband, from the man who would one day be laird. It held all the weight and authority of the position and her mind told her to listen, but her heart couldn't.

"Nae. Ye canne go out there alone." She leaned in and dug her head into his shoulder, shaking it back and forth.

"I willnae be alone. He is surrounded and has naewhere to go." Grant gave her another small kiss. "Trust me."

"I do trust ye. I dinnae trust Torsten." A knock sounded from the closed door.

"I need to go now." He ran his fingers through her hair. "I love ye, Isobel."

She wanted to say it, her mouth even parted, but fear intruded. He let go and was leaving. He wasn't going to come back. Somehow, she knew if she said it right now, she would never see him again.

Then he was gone, and the door closed behind him. A key scraped into place on the other side and she heard a click as the bolt on the door locked into place, pinning her in as fear wound its way around her heart.

About half an hour later, she stopped at the window to inspect the rain as she deliberated what to do. A crushing weight pressed on her chest and she couldn't breathe, which reminded her of the man sitting on her all those years ago.

A boat crossing the divide between Skye and the mainland slid gracefully across the waters. It was almost eerie, given the clouds still roiling in the sky despite the reprieve from the heavy rains.

Panic took hold.

She ran to the door and started banging on it. "Help."

"'Tis all right, Isobel," came a voice from the other side. Ian.

"Ye have to let me out. Torsten will kill him. He cannae be trusted."

"Grant isnae going alone. There are more than a hundred men over there to keep him safe."

"Nae, ye have to let me out."

"I cannae do that, lass. I have orders."

She pounded on the door again, but Ian ignored her.

Stepping over to her dressing table she reminded herself to think. Her lungs threatened to seize as she fought the helplessness. She was going to fight back. This wouldn't be like before.

The pendant Grant's mother had given her caught her eye. This was her family now. She belonged here with the MacDonalds, with Grant. She was a MacDonald and their laird's heir needed help.

Sliding the ruby and pearl inlaid MacDonald crest on, she cleared her panic and prepared to do battle.

She grabbed a pen knife used for sharpening writing instruments then knelt at the door. Her rose-colored gown bunched around her like petals on a delicate flower. She cursed there was no better option for dressing, but all of her men's clothing had been taken and she'd become accustomed to the excess material.

After sliding the pointed end of the knife into the keyhole, she closed her eyes to concentrate. She'd never been good at picking locks, but if her husband ever did this to her again, she would become the best lockpick in all of Scotland. The instrument just fit and shortly she heard a *click*.

The door flew in as she pulled, and she came face-to-face with her husband's best friend.

When the bigger man blocked her way, she stood her ground. "Torsten is going to kill him. Ye have to get me over there."

"What makes ye think that? Grant is taking him a fortune."

How did they not know? "He doesnae desire riches."

"Everyone wants coin."

"Torsten has all the coin he needs. The only thing he

wishes is the recognition of his cousin, the Earl of Argyll. Turning me over is the only way he'll get that. Ye have to trust me, Ian. He's in danger." Moisture pooled in her eyes. "Ye ken I can defend myself."

"Aye."

"And ye ken I am just as prepared as all those men out there to fight in battle."

Ian sighed and ran a hand through his hair.

"Let's go save him. Come with me."

He still looked reluctant.

"If ye dinnae take me, I'll break my neck scaling the wall or will drown in the water. The only way ye can protect me is to see me safely to his side."

Ian must have seen the truth of her resolve because he nodded. Stepping aside, he let her enter the hall as she said, "We'll need weapons."

•••

As the shore grew closer, Grant thought through the plan one more time. MacDonald men had been dispatched from farther up the coastline to avoid detection, and to cover any means of escape. There were easily a hundred men in strategic locations.

Some had also been sent to their kin of Clanranald to inform them the meeting would take place on their land, and it was a Campbell who wished the clan harm.

Strolling up to the tavern on the outskirts of the village where Torsten wanted to meet, Grant scanned the surroundings, looking for any threats. His men had thoroughly searched the inn last night and had been keeping watch since then to be certain Torsten was alone.

Isobel had insisted Grant couldn't trust Torsten Campbell and he respected her instincts, but he had to see if they could come to an agreement without bloodshed. In addition to the many MacDonald men who had the surroundings covered, he'd brought Owen, Boyd, and another of his friends along to provide assistance should conversation turn to violence. The men would wait just outside the door. They'd agreed upon a sharp whistle as a call sign for trouble should the need for immediate assistance arrive.

Upon reaching the front, he waited for the signal to indicate Torsten was alone. The bird call came and Grant pulled open the door.

His boots hammered out assurance and defiance as he strode across the room to the man sitting alone at a table with his back to the wall.

A young family occupied one table, wet clothes clinging to them. One man sat at another table topped with a tray holding a pitcher and overflowing plates of a stew. A group of men eyed him from the corner—their presence was unexpected. Other than that, the room was clear.

He dragged a chair across the floor to take a seat. Torsten Campbell's cold scrutiny was almost unreadable, with only a hint of annoyance escaping the corners of his mouth as he leaned back and crossed his arms. His eyes were blue, a color so light it reminded him of ice that hung from the edge of a roof in winter.

"Campbell." He'd only briefly seen the man during the melee months earlier, but he had noticed the scar that ran through the man's eyebrow, cutting it in half.

One of the children complained, "'Tis cold, Mother. I dinnae like it." The outburst reminded him that there were innocents in the room.

Grant focused on the threat in front of him, but he leaned back to ensure he could still see the other men from the corner of his eye.

"Where is she?" Anger dripped from the arse's mouth,

the last word ground out between clenched teeth.

"I've come to make ye an offer of peace."

"What do you propose?" Torsten picked at his nails, seeming to relax as a smirk turned up the thick lines of his lips.

After removing the bag from his shoulder, Grant untied the top and placed it in the middle of the table, peeling back the folds of fabric to reveal gold coins.

Torsten reached into the bag, pulled out a small handful, and held it out palm up. "This is what ye offer."

"Aye. 'Tis a fortune. And I offer protection for ye as long as ye live on MacDonald lands. Ye will never want for anything." He didn't have to tell Torsten that if he tried to leave Skye, the man would pay with his life. As it was, he was going to be lucky to live through this day.

The man's fingers closed around the gold, his knuckles whitening. Despite his face remaining passive, Grant could tell there was a shift in Torsten's mood. The air thickened around Grant as he realized Isobel had been correct. There wasn't going to be a pleasant ending.

Torsten flicked his wrists, pelting Grant in the face with the coins. Small stings hit his skin and he rose, his chair *thunking* to the floor. One of the children called out, and their parents bundled them through the door. *Good*. The family would be safe, and his men would know the negotiations had not ended well.

Once the family had cleared the room, he addressed the red-faced menace in front of him.

Torsten had also jumped to his feet, along with the men in the corner, while the cook and the server appeared from the kitchens to join their ranks.

Hell, where had they all come from? The MacDonalds had thoroughly checked the inn ahead of time, making certain the only one who entered was Torsten, but he'd managed to sneak in a small group.

"I dinnae want yer coin or to live with a clan other than the Campbells. I want the wench."

"She is a MacDonald now. Ye cannae have her."

"Ye would risk the wrath of the Earl of Argyll to protect her? She is a criminal."

"My clan has already suffered the notice of the earl. Let him come to Skye. Ye yerself wouldnae breach our shores. He doesnae stand a chance." Grant shuddered, thinking of the earl's ire directly on them, but they had allies and if it were to be war, he'd call on them to rise up and defeat the Covenanters with Clan MacDonald. Besides, these men were surrounded and wouldn't make it back to the Covenanter leader.

"I want Isobel."

"Ye cannae have her. Take the money and offer." He needed to somehow draw the men outside where his men were waiting—he couldn't take them all in this small space.

The men at the table and the two who had come in through the kitchen drew their swords, ready to pounce. "If ye touch me, ye willnae make it home alive. We have ye surrounded."

"Then we will take ye until we have the wench and are safe on our own lands. The MacDonald willnae let harm befall his only heir." Torsten nodded his head to the men.

Grant reached for the knife at his side and pursed his lips to give the whistle, but before a sound emerged a stinging pain slammed the back of his head. As the room blurred, he saw the tavern servant swinging a club. He fell to his knees.

"Bring him," Torsten said as the men rounded the table, moving toward him. "Let's show the MacDonalds what they'll lose if they don't hand over the wench." A boot jabbed his ribs, shooting pain through his already dazed senses.

Then arms were around his shoulders, dragging him back out into the waning light.

Chapter Twenty-Three

After securing a sword from the wall in the great hall then stopping by the kitchen to retrieve an extra dirk from one of the cooks, Isobel and Ian made their way down the winding steps to the shore. She didn't care who saw them. She wanted Torsten's attention on her instead of her husband.

The courtyard and grounds were eerily quiet, and she wasn't sure if it was because an army of MacDonalds had gone to take care of the threat, or if the men who usually loitered about were inside because of the weather that was slowly clearing.

"Ye ken Grant is going to kill me if anything happens to ye," Ian said as he pushed a small fishing vessel into the water.

"Are ye sure that thing will see us across?" She had doubts whether the boat would float, given the size and deterioration of the boards. She was also certain Ian was moving slow in order to ensure any conflict that arose would be ended before she could arrive.

"Aye. 'Twill move swift and nae leave me aching with fatigue by the time we reach the other shore."

Ian and she spent the rest of the trip devising a plan as he filled her in on the location of all MacDonald men who had been sent to accompany Grant. Chances were all was settled already, but she had to know he was safe. The crushing weight on her chest wouldn't go away. It was irrational, but she couldn't trust anyone else to protect him.

Midway across the water, the drizzle ceased and the clouds parted to reveal the golden rays of the sun. Warmth spread over her skin, not from comfort but dread. She would defend Grant with her last breath if that's what it took.

Ian used a large rope to tie off the boat then nodded in the direction of the tavern. "I'll be right here with ye. I willnae let anything happen this time." She guessed he'd been left behind because of his head injury, but Ian seemed to think he'd let Grant down and was attempting to make up for the incident in Edinburgh.

"He doesnae blame ye. Ye ken that?"

Ian took in a deep breath. "We'll see what happens when he finds out I brought ye here."

"Then stay close and I'll let him ken how ye saved me from falling to my death from Cairntay's walls."

A few moments later, she caught a glimpse of the building, but just as Ian and she had discussed, she skirted around to the back where she would wait until he had determined whether Grant was safe. The MacDonald men motioned for her to back down, but she pressed forward to find a better hiding spot closer to the door. Their movements, however, were enough of a distraction that she tripped over something solid on the ground.

A body.

Three bodies. The forms didn't look like MacDonald warriors. One man was overweight, the second was mere bones, the third was an older woman, an apron tied around her waist. It had to be the owners of the tavern.

What was going on in there?

Her chest caved in and ice formed in her veins. Was Grant in there by himself?

The sound of a woman screaming and children crying came as she scrambled to her feet, pulled up her skirts, and ran for the building. She could only hope Grant had not gone in there alone, and that he'd been prepared to fight. Her heart plummeted when the back door slammed open, and two men dragged a dazed Grant from the tavern.

Torsten emerged next, a devious smile on his lips. The smirk only intensified when he met her gaze then scanned the small clearing. Somehow, she found the courage to motion toward the woods, signaling Ian and the others to stand down. Otherwise, she wouldn't be able to bargain with the man in front of her.

"Well, look who we have here." Torsten stepped forward and she pulled the small sword from the sheath at her side. It was more like hers and would be easier to wield than Ian's had been.

"Dinnae come closer."

"Ye do look quite bonny now that yer not dressed like a man with dirt on yer face. There must be something good under that skirt. Ye should have seen the gold this fool was offering to keep ye."

One of the men beside Grant held up a bag and smiled with a row of broken and missing teeth.

Defying her warning, Torsten took a step, his eyes darkening. "I may have to see what's so special about ye on the way to hand ye over to my cousin."

Grant attempted to get to his feet, a combination of pain and fear etched in his eyes. "Nae, Isobel, get out…"

One of the men punched her husband in his belly and he collapsed on the ground. A flashback of her maid Morna doing the same, just before she'd been assaulted, stabbed at her memory.

"Let him go."

"Now why would I do that? He's been harboring a fugitive." Torsten's tongue darted out, wetting his lips.

Save Grant first then the baby.

"Take me instead. Let him go, and I'll turn myself over willingly." Getting Grant to safety was the only thing that mattered. Ian had reluctantly agreed the life of the MacDonald heir was crucial to their clan and his well-being had to come first. Although he waited only yards behind her, she trusted him to stay back. It was the other MacDonald men who might mess up the plan.

"Nae," Grant roared, but she couldn't look at him.

"I think I'll take ye both."

"If ye kill him, the MacDonalds will never let ye live. Take me, and ye have a shot at making it home." She had to speed this up before someone else showed. She couldn't take all the men, but Ian was here, and she could see others flanking the area. All she had to do was take out Torsten.

"Nae, Isobel, ye cannae do this." Grant somehow found it in his voice to make the words sound like an order, even as he struggled to win free from the men holding him.

"If ye kill him there will be a war." She took a step toward Torsten. When he said nothing, she continued, "Ye must decide quick. There are others coming, and they willnae let ye go."

"She's telling the truth," Torsten's man holding a massive club called out. "If ye kill the MacDonald heir, we are all doomed. Take her and let's go."

She threw her sword down. "I willnae fight ye."

"Do ye think me a fool, lass? 'Twill nae be yer only weapon."

She could do this. She would sacrifice herself for Grant.

"Have yer men step away from him, and I'll give them all

up. I have to ken he is safe."

"Isobel," Grant fumed.

"The clan needs ye. They dinnae need me." Tears stung the back of her eyes. She'd never told him what he meant to her. She'd never said the words, and now it would be too late. So he wouldn't see her regret, she remained focused on Torsten.

At the nod of the Campbell in charge, his men backed away, keeping swords drawn in case Grant rose up. "Stay," one of them ordered her husband and was met with projected fury so intense she saw the man shudder from this distance.

"Now, the rest of yer weapons."

She reached behind her back, withdrew the dirk she'd slipped into the laces of the gown, and tossed it down in front of her.

"I ken that's not all."

"I'll get rid of the last one, but ye all have to take another step away from Grant."

Torsten nodded, moving to only a few paces away. He'd be on her before she had a chance to react if she gave it up too soon.

She pointed. "Tell them to back away."

"Do as she says," he ordered. "We'll let the man go."

Once they did, she pulled up the edge of her skirt and removed the *sgian-dubh* she had strapped to her stockings. "That's all." She tossed it into the pile.

"Untie the horses," Torsten called over his shoulder as he grabbed her by the arm. A man holding a large sack started to work on the horses she'd seen behind the tavern. Then, he turned back to the other men. "Kill him."

"Nae," she screamed as her heart fell from her chest.

• • •

Despair overwhelmed Grant when Isobel offered herself over to the Campbell bastard. What would the Earl of Argyll do to her?

Damn, and she was with his child. He had to protect both of them. He'd spent most of his adulthood avoiding confrontation, but he would do whatever it took to keep his family safe. If he lost them, he lost everything.

He straightened his shoulders. A tug in his side confirmed he might have a broken rib, but he could fight through the pain. He just had to get his stubborn wife free. When he got her to safety, he was going to bend her over his knee, and he would skewer Ian for letting her out.

His gut twisted in knots, but he tamped it down. She needed him to keep a clear head. The men he'd brought with him were nearby, and the ones his father had sent earlier would cut off the Campbells' escape. The MacDonalds would be on them before Torsten could get far.

The man was a shrewd arse, obviously determined to gain the admiration of the leader of the Covenanter forces. What if the bastard felt trapped and decided the next best thing to turning over the woman of the Resistance was killing her? Or just as bad, if he realized he couldn't escape, he might try to take her down with him, just because he could.

Despite her abilities, Isobel was at a severe disadvantage. The Campbell man was large and while he didn't have a weapon drawn, he carried several on him.

His gaze drifting around the group, he assessed each man, noting what his earlier mistake had been. The one who stood just a few yards away holding a hefty club had been the server. The haphazard assortment on the tray and the cold food should have been an indication something wasn't right. He'd assumed the servant was a member of Clanranald, and he cursed himself for not recognizing the threat.

The faint call of a robin reached his ears, a sound that

had become second nature, one that brought comfort and security. Then another, so low the Campbell men paid no heed. Another and then yet one more. The signal his men were in striking position and had cut off any means of escape. They wouldn't let anything happen to Isobel.

Just as Torsten Campbell ordered his death, Ian emerged from behind a tree in perfect unison with Owen, Boyd, and Joseph. The men split the air with a battle cry, pulling attention away from him. He ignored the pain in his side and rose up to his full height.

Ian dashed forward and tossed a sword in his direction. Grant caught it by the hilt, just before the man who had punched him in his rib swung his claymore, aiming for the spot he'd kicked. Not yet having a solid grip due to the broad sword's basket hilt, Grant swerved to avoid the blow, twirling and retreating to give himself time to adjust his fingering and gauge the confrontation.

All the Campbell men were covered, except for Torsten, who, instead of going for his weapon, struggled to keep a grip on a determined Isobel as she fought with the arse. Knowing she was safe for the moment, he focused on the man barreling toward him.

As his opponent swung, Grant noticed the slightly younger brute was skilled but impatient. He'd likely trained for several years, but had never seen real battle. He deflected the blow but nearly overcompensated with the unfamiliar sword. The sound of clashing metal rended the air, followed by the high-pitched squeal of the weapons sliding off each other.

His attacker recovered, gracefully returning to an offensive stance, ready to strike again. Grant did the same. And waited. Despite the straight posture and attention to the fight, a tremor shook his opponent's hands. The man's gaze darted about, likely searching for a means of escape or for reinforcements. There would be no help coming—the MacDonalds would have found and eliminated them by now.

This man appeared as if he might see reason, but unfortunately for him, time for negotiations and truces had passed.

No Campbell would ever return and threaten his wife. This ended today.

Now.

He swung. The brute raised his claymore to meet the strike, the weapons bouncing off each other with the force. Vibrations moved through his palm and up to his shoulder.

The Campbell man thrust again, lower and on the opposite side. Grant blocked it, but as he twisted to get into position, his side erupted in pain.

Pushing forward anyway, he volleyed another strike. It missed as the man danced out of reach. Another blow, this time up high, and Grant easily avoided it. One more in the same pattern was deflected, and the brute stumbled backward, winded. But Grant realized his surroundings had blurred. He had to blink to bring it back into focus, just as another assault came toward his midsection.

He blocked it, but his sword slid across the other and the man's blade just missed his arm. Taking a deep breath, he tried to clear the numb feeling that invaded as their battle continued. It was getting worse with each movement.

He had to end this soon or risk real injury. He struck, fast and furious, swinging down with as much force as he could produce. The blow was deflected, but it had the desired effect—the man wobbled and almost lost control of his blade.

Grant didn't give him time to recover, coming in low on the opposite side, hitting his mark then slicing into the man's thigh. His opponent yelped then tried to catch Grant in the back, but he was prepared and already swinging down and across the man's belly, where he connected when his sharp blade penetrated cloth then skin.

Claymore falling to the ground, the man tried to stop the red spilling from his gut, but the flow was too fast. The brute collapsed in the mud. Grant kicked him to make certain he was no longer a threat just as he heard the bastard holding Isobel scream, "Ye crazy wench."

Icy dread impaled him when he saw crimson staining her arm and covering the front of her gown. Torsten glared at her as he jerked his hand high. The arse struck her with a closed fist and she staggered then fell to her knees while the man went for his sword.

Chapter Twenty-Four

Losing her battle to free herself of Torsten's grip, Isobel shouted, "Ye willnae make it out of here alive."

"Then neither will yer husband." With his free hand, he pulled out a pistol. Her throat closed and she couldn't breathe as he raised the weapon and aimed at Grant, who was currently obscured behind the man he was fighting.

With no weapons and not able to reach Torsten's knife, she struggled more furiously so he couldn't aim at her husband. While flailing, she unfastened the pin on the back of her necklace and prayed it would be sharp and long enough to do some damage.

After disengaging the clasp, she clenched it in her fist, pin protruding from her fingers, and stabbed Torsten's neck, the chain just giving her enough slack to reach him. The tip pierced the sensitive spot just below his ear, sinking in, and his whole body tensed.

Her weapon was small, but she'd aimed for the place Alex had taught her. "When ye are desperate, strike here."

Blood gushed from the wound, covering her hand then

spilling onto the front of her gown before she had a chance to withdraw.

Torsten's grip loosened and he dropped his gun when he clasped his neck to stop the flow. She was about to dive for one of his weapons when he struck her and she stumbled. Blinded with pain, she fell to her knees while Torsten drew his sword and sliced toward her.

Flinching, she ducked her head, as if the small gesture would be enough to save her from the killing blow. At the clash of metal, she looked up to find Grant standing between Torsten and her and had blocked the strike, saving her life.

"I gave ye the chance to live a good life."

"I amnae going back without her."

"'Tis true, because ye willnae be going back at all." The pure rage that spewed from Grant's lips sent chills through her—the warrior taking over, suppressing the man who sought peace at all costs. And for the first time since she and her maid had been attacked as children, she felt protected and had faith someone else would keep her safe. She wanted to cry with the blessed peace that washed over her.

Torsten held his sword aloft, planting his feet solidly on the ground. Desperation and fury sparked in his eyes—the man obviously knew he was done for and his only option was to take out as many of them as he could before he went down. She'd seen it before. That's when men truly became dangerous.

And if she didn't move now, her husband might trip over her, giving Torsten a chance at a killing blow.

Unable to crawl in her skirts, she dove and rolled to the side, muck spattering on her dress. At a safe distance, she stumbled to her feet as Ian appeared and pulled her farther away. He called out to Grant, "I've got her."

She made out his slight nod as he stared at Torsten. Grant swayed slightly as he moved into position to brace against the Campbell bastard's first blow. Her husband was apparently injured, but Torsten still clutched at the side of his neck and struck with one hand holding his claymore. Grant easily deflected the strike and followed through, nearly knocking the arse's weapon from his hand.

"She's a criminal," Torsten spat.

"Nae. She is my wife, and ye will never lay another hand on her." Although she couldn't see Grant's face, she heard the confidence as her husband's shoulders straightened.

Moving his hand from the neck wound, Torsten clasped his blade with both hands. Blood gushed from the spot, staining his once pristine shirt. After thrusting his claymore forward, a clang erupted as the metal collided, and both men stumbled back with the force.

Seconds passed as each tried to anticipate the other's next move. Everything slowed as Torsten hurled his sword at Grant, pivoted, and bolted toward her, drawing his knife as he lunged forward.

Ian pulled her back, and the other MacDonald men appeared between her and the attacker, shielding her just as Grant tackled him to the soft ground.

Grant and Torsten struggled to stand. Her heart stung with fear and helplessness upon seeing Grant's pale face as he wobbled before gaining his footing.

Torsten lunged with the knife in his blood-soaked hand, but Grant ducked and blocked the blow. The weapon slipped from the arse's grip and tumbled to the earth. Grant punched Torsten's cheek and he stumbled. Grant struck again and again. One last time, and the man she'd feared would harm her friends, family, and husband, collapsed to the ground.

She ran for Grant, throwing her arms around him as the stinging in her eyes gave way to a trail of tears down her face. His arms circled her, holding her tight, wrapping her in security and warmth. He hugged her like he believed he'd never see her again. Not wanting to move, she held on with abandon, not caring what went on in the world around them, confident that the rest of the MacDonald men were keeping an eye on Torsten to ensure he posed no more danger.

Grant staggered, almost losing his balance.

She stepped back. "Are ye hurt?" Placing her hands on his head, she gazed into his eyes. They were glazed over and his pupils were dilated, indicating he'd not escaped the day without injury.

"'Twill be all right when I get ye home." He tightened his hold on her. "I'm tempted to lock ye and Ian up in the dungeon for no' listening to me."

"Ye might be dead if we hadn't come."

"Aye, but I would have kenned ye were safe. I thought ye were gone when ye offered yerself for me. If ye ever do anything like that again, ye'll never be allowed to leave Cairntay."

"I dinnae want to leave anyway. As long as ye are there, I have everything I need. I have ye and our baby to watch over now. 'Tis all I want." She took in the carnage, but also the MacDonald men who had put her safety first. And she trusted her bairn and she would be protected.

There was nowhere else she wanted to be but at her husband's side, with Clan MacDonald at her back.

The smile that came to Grant's lips warmed her heart, reminding her that he had become everything. She blinked slowly, her heart racing as she let the emotion spill from her soul. "I love ye, Grant MacDonald."

He inhaled and for a second she worried she had cursed them, that giving voice to what she'd been feeling these last few weeks would destroy her.

"Say it again." He took her hands and peered into her eyes, intensity erasing the clouds in his gaze.

She swallowed. "I love ye."

Then, he was pulling her in, coiling his arms around her as his mouth claimed hers in a kiss that said he felt the same.

Epilogue

Grant woke to a slight pressure on his chest. It then nudged his cheek. Opening his eyes, he stared at the little furr ball meowing at him, vying for his attention. He smiled then turned onto his side to glance at his wife. She still had a slight bruising on her face where Torsten Campbell had struck her, but knowing the man and his crew lay buried in the cold earth and would never hurt another was some comfort.

When he'd seen the man's sword aimed at Isobel kneeling helpless on the ground, he'd known sheer panic, the kind that had stopped his heart. He was certain he would relive that moment in nightmares for the rest of his life. He would thank God every day he'd been fast enough to block the blow.

He had her here now, and she insisted she was done with the Resistance and wanted nothing more than to stay on Skye and keep their bairn safe. He'd even penned an anonymous letter to Alex Gordon yesterday to let the man know she was done with that life and to make sure he never came to seek her out.

The lass willnae be returning to yer ranks. The threat has been eliminated. Please inform those that ye come across that the woman of the Resistance is dead. Thank ye for looking after her in the past. She is no longer yer concern.

Isobel said as long as she had use of the lists and could train the MacDonald women to protect themselves she would be happy. He would let her have that. She'd already taught Annis how to use a *sgian-dubh*.

After failing to gain his attention, Daracha pounced on Isobel. Her eyes flew open and she looked around in panic until her gaze rested on his.

"Tell me again," he whispered to her as he pushed a curl back from her cheek.

The corners of her lips curved up and her sleepy smile nearly melted his heart. "I love ye, husband."

And he knew no matter what came, war or peace, prosperity or famine, he would have her by his side and everything would be right with the world.

Author's Note

While the characters in the *Highland Pride* series are fictional, the conflict of the times is rooted in facts. Here is a brief history of the actual events surrounding the tumultuous relationship between England and Scotland and peoples of different faiths.

The reign of King Charles I lasted from 1625 to 1649. The grandson of the famed Mary, Queen of Scots, he was only the second monarch to rule over Scotland, Ireland, and England. Although raised Protestant, he believed in the divine right of kings, which did not sit well with the English Parliament who vied for more control. He further enraged Parliament by marrying Henrietta Maria of France, a Roman Catholic.

Thinking to bring Scotland and England closer together in their customs, in 1637, Charles attempted to impose an Anglican-style common book of prayer in Scotland. This angered the Protestants in Scotland, because the Scottish church had different practices and doctrines from the English church.

This led to an incident where, it is said, Jenny Geddes, a merchant or tradesperson from Edinburgh, threw a stool at the minister in St. Giles Cathedral during the first use of the *Booke Of Prayer*. This was the start of chaos that broke out within the congregation. There is some debate as to whether she was one of a number of women who had been paid to arrive early and disrupt the service.

Officers were summoned and unruly churchgoers were escorted from the building. Jenny Geddes's actions are believed to have spurred rioting in the streets, where the ejected parishioners beat on the doors and threw rocks at the windows. This riot is believed to be what led to the Wars of the Three Kingdoms, which is sometimes referred to as the British Civil Wars, including the English Civil War.

In February of 1638, the first National Covenant objecting to Charles's prayer book was circulated and signed by many nobles in Scotland. In November of that year, the Scottish Parliament became Presbyterian and expelled all the bishops and archbishops from the Church of Scotland. Charles reacted to the insult by launching the Bishops War.

Flames were added to the mix when the Cambridge Press was established by Puritans in 1638. There, they were able to print Puritan propaganda against the king and further deepen the divide in England.

On August 7, 1643, an additional covenant was agreed upon by the Scottish Covenanters then sent to the Church of Scotland, which accepted it on the twenty-fifth of the same month. This was during the first English Civil War, when England was trying to garner support from Scotland in their bid to oust King Charles. The Solemn League and Covenant was accepted by the Westminster Assembly and English Parliament on September 25, 1643.

Charles I was executed after the second English Civil War and his son, Charles the II, was persuaded to sign the agreement. In 1661, the Solemn League and Covenant was declared unlawful by the English Parliament.

Acknowledgments

Special thanks to:

Robin Haseltine, for her guidance and diligent attention to detail, her continued faith in me, and all the hard work and time she has dedicated to making the *Highland Pride* series the best it can be. She is a truly gifted editor.

Jessica Watterson, who will drop other things to have wine and cheese with me. She has been my advocate and sounding board. Fate found a way to bring us together, despite my poor choice in footwear, and I will be forever grateful she is my agent.

My best friend, my husband, for his love, support, and for understanding when the story calls and I forget what we're talking about, that I still love him, and he will always be my real-life hero.

My kids and my parents, Jo Ann and David Bailey, for encouraging me and being proud of what I do.

Eliza Knight and Madeline Martin, for keeping me motivated and sane. I treasure our special bond and how we support each other every day.

My writing tribe, for sharing their enthusiasm, love of the craft, and wisdom along with keeping me motivated and on track. I will always be eternally grateful to: Michele Sandiford, Harper Kincaid, Denny S. Bryce, Jennifer McKeone, Nadine Monaco, Keely Thrall, Gabriel Ross, Jessica Snyder, and everyone in WRWDC.

And as always, for you, the reader, who picked up this book and gave me a chance to share a piece of my heart.

About the Author

Lori Ann Bailey is a lover of wine, country music, and chocolate. When she was around ten, she dreamed of becoming a country singer. She even penned her own song, but her brothers soon informed her that she didn't possess the vocal range to follow that dream. Eventually, she entered the business world where she worked as an assistant buyer before becoming a stay-at-home mom. In order to meet people when she moved to a new neighborhood, she joined two book clubs.

When she picked up that first book, something unexpected happened. She was hooked. Lori started reading for pleasure, only to discover she'd always had her own private reality dancing in her head. After convincing her husband to purchase a laptop, she began typing the bedtime tales she'd told herself since childhood. Now she writes novels to tell others her stories, just as she had in the song she'd written so many years earlier.

Winner of the National Readers' Choice Award and Holt Medallion for Best First Book and Best Historical, Lori writes hunky Highland heroes and strong-willed independent lasses finding their perfect matches in the Highlands of 17th century Scotland.

She has served two years as the Washington DC Romance Writers Program Director and is currently on her second stint of service to Romance Writers of America as a member of the National Workshop Committee. She's also a founding member of the blog RomanceontheRocks.com and a contributor to the podcast, *History, Books, and Wine.*

After growing up and attending college in Mississippi, she lived in Ohio, Manhattan, and London, but chose to settle in Vienna, VA with her husband and four children. When not writing or reading, Lori enjoys time with her real-life hero and four kids or spending time walking or drinking wine with her friends.

Visit Lori Ann Bailey in the following places:

http://loriannbailey.com/ — be sure to sign up for her newsletter for exclusive content and so you don't miss any news.

https://www.facebook.com/LoriAnnBaileyauthor/
https://www.bookbub.com/profile/lori-ann-bailey
https://www.goodreads.com/LoriAnnBailey
https://www.amazon.com/Lori-Ann-Bailey/e/B01JGPBQSO
https://www.instagram.com/loriannbailey/

Don't miss the Highland Pride series...

HIGHLAND DECEPTION

HIGHLAND REDEMPTION

HIGHLAND TEMPTATION

HIGHLAND SALVATION

Discover more Amara titles...

A LADY NEVER TELLS
a *Women Daring* novel by Lynn Winchester

When Richard Downing, a viscount of impeccable character, stumbles upon a housemaid with a dagger hidden in her skirts, color him intrigued. Lady Victoria Daring is full of secrets and surprises, first and foremost that she is a master of disguises sent to infiltrate high society for the Crown. Richard is the first man to see through her disguises—and infiltrate deep into her heart. Too bad his family is at the top of her list of suspects...

WHAT A SCOT WANTS
a novel by Amalie Howard and Angie Morgan

Highlander Ronan Maclaren is in no hurry to marry. And he hasn't found the right woman. Lady Imogen has avoided wedlock for years. Determined to remain independent, she makes herself unattractive to all suitors. When a betrothal contract is signed—unbeknownst to Ronan or Imogen—it's loathing at first sight. They each vow to make the other cry off—by any means necessary. But what starts out as a battle of wits... quickly dissolves into a battle of wills.

SAVING THE SCOT
a *Highlanders of Balforss* novel by Jennifer Trethewey

Louisa's father is shipping her off to America to marry a stranger, so she concocts a plan to switch places with her maid. Highlander Ian Sinclair needs an army commission, and the only way he can get one is to deliver Louisa to America. Just when Louisa thinks her plan has worked, with no one the wiser...Ian discovers her secret, and all hell breaks loose.

Printed in the USA
CPSIA information can be obtained
at www.ICGtesting.com
LVHW091530101023
760699LV00002B/208

9 781692 813291